Lardeux

OUT of the WILD NIGHT

OUT of the WILD NIGHT

Blue Balliett

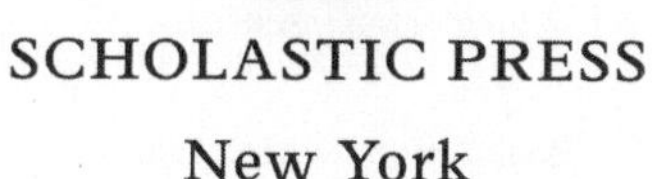

SCHOLASTIC PRESS
New York

Library of Congress Cataloging-in-Publication Data available

ISBN 978-0-545-86756-6

10 9 8 7 6 5 4 3 2 1 18 19 20 21 22

Printed in the U.S.A. 23
First edition, April 2018

Book design by Abby Dening

For Bill

It is good for a man to invite his ghosts . . .
out of the wild night, into the firelight,
out of the howling dark.

—A. S. Byatt

I am not what I am, I am what I do
with my hands.

—Louise Bourgeois

Am I walking toward something
I should be running away from?

—Shirley Jackson

CHAPTER 1

The Crier is here. Ding, ding!

My story begins at dusk, on the edges, by the shore and around the graveyards. Let me tell you, this is a Nantucket November like no other.

On the good side of being in my current state is that time works like the pages of a book made from fog or snow. You can flip this way or that and things are always changing order. Flowing. Regrouping around the motion of your hand.

On the bad side?

Being dead.

But wait, that may not be all bad. Being dead has its advantages, especially around here.

My name is Mary. Mary W. Chase. Chase as in *Run, I might be behind you*!

I died one hundred years ago, plus a few days.

Today I was shaken awake. A tremendous rumbling, a roar of vibrations, jolted me back from wherever I've been. I don't remember dying, nor do I remember what happened immediately after.

I wake, I sleep; I wake, I sleep—such is the life of someone like me.

Just now I was tossed back with no warning into the rough, pitch-and-tumble world of the living.

Wait, don't move! I feel danger everywhere, a rush of fear that we who've lived know well—an awareness that all might be over in a pounce. A prickling. Am I alone?

I try my voice, but don't know if it makes a sound anyone else can hear. "Hello," I whisper. "Hellohellohelloooo!" Louder this time.

A board creaks beneath my feet. I look down but see nothing.

I've been resting, present but not, inside the walls of my old home, happy in the familiar company of wood and plaster. Free of worry. Settled.

Being a curious but shy soul in life—a watcher and a spy—I always did wonder how an egg could be so perfect and yet so easily broken. Life is miraculous but fragile, filled with risk and danger—and is death, too?

B-BAM! Rrrroar! What is the noise I'm hearing? Is it the end of all we know?

"Help!" I gasp. If I'm already dead, why should I hold back? "Help me, someone!" I call out, louder this time.

My voice creaks like a rusted hinge.

Does *anyone* hear me? "HELP!"

Two children pass by my front window. I rap on the glass, but neither one turns to look. The girl has hair like seaweed, all dark ripples, and the boy is the color of sand.

RRRoarrrr! The grinding and rattling start again. The girl and boy clap their hands over their ears. My heart sinks.

"Helphelphelp!" I yell, surely loud enough to wake the world.

No answer. The children walk quickly and don't glance back.

Now I recognize my fingers, pressed against the window. I wiggle my toes and look down to see dark stockings. And there! My boots are by the door. I'm no longer invisible, at least to myself.

But why am I here?

It must be the children.

~

I once lived in this town and still do, although I'm no longer the one who sweeps mud and horse dung from the front steps of my home. My rotten teeth no longer bother me. I realize now that I'm back as the island's Town Crier, a bold job I was much too timid to have done when living. *Crying* doesn't mean *weeping* here; it means *calling out*. I'll ring my handbell for attention and shout the news through a copper horn.

We Criers can be loud.

In my day, Nantucket had a living Town Crier, a famous and skinny man who walked up and down our streets and lanes, making an endless amount of noise.

His name was Billy Clark.

Everyone stopped to listen. We'd hear when a boat was on its way into the harbor, if a person was born or had just died, where to buy wool, fresh mutton, or salted cod. Since we didn't have any other way to share instant news, the Crier was essential.

In life, I spoke only when spoken to. I was guarded inside and pleasant on the outside. I kept my skirts tucked close and my hair pinned tight. My mouth was as small as a flounder's and my eyes were step-on-me pebbles. My entire family died one year in a terrible fever when I was young, and I was taken in by a grumpy aunt. I soon married a silent man, the first who asked. My husband, Daniel, was a lifelong fisherman who hardly noticed me. We never had children, but I kept that sadness tucked in the pockets of my apron. Over and over, I scrubbed and baked. I wanted to be heard and cherished, but wasn't.

I never dreamed I'd become so important one day. The Town Crier! Am I back in order to warn?

As I look around my home, the floorboards vibrate beneath my feet and the walls shiver. What monsters lurk outside?

"Billy," I call out, joking but not. "You can keep your job!"

No reply.

CHAPTER 2

We tip

If I had bones, they'd be rattling like dried beans in a bowl. Perhaps Maushop wants to take back his gritty slipper.

As a child, I heard an old Wampanoag Indian legend about a giant by the name of Maushop, a man of huge size who lived on the mainland. One day, he got sand in his moccasins. First he kicked off one to form Martha's Vineyard, an island close to shore. Then off went the other moccasin in irritation, forming Nantucket, which means *faraway island*.

There are still quiet moments in my home, almost too quiet. No creaking of carriage wheels or jingle-clop of horses outside. And then *WHAM!* All shakes and roars.

Maushop, is that you?

Wait, let me peek from my window again. The street

is deliciously familiar and yet not. All slides fast, in flashes, the colors slipping by impossibly bright and smooth, like boiled icing on a cake. I see the red of a ripe cranberry, the yellow of a Christmas lemon—noisy machines known as cars and trucks, new to the world when I was old. Is *that* what I heard? Nearby gardens look to be on their best behavior. Homes are framed by hedges as tidy as a bridegroom's haircut.

I touch the wooden silk of my windowsill and the worn brick around my fireplace. I feel the hum of living surround me. My blue-and-white teapot is still on a shelf; the old woman who lived here after me liked to watch for children and to bake and fry, as I did. I can picture a plate of sugar doughnuts—we called them *wonders*—cooling inside the door.

The kitchen has water that pours out in the sink, both hot and cold. The outhouse in back of the kitchen is gone, leaving small rooms for doing your business inside. No spiders. No cleanup. I love the boxes that make a churning noise and scrub clothes and crockery and even dry them.

In my house! What a miracle for all who do the chores!

But there are other changes that are hard. Back I go to the window, and spread my fingers flat against the panes as the earth shakes again.

It's time to step outside. I clang my bell and shout. This is harder than you'd think.

As I walk down my street, I sense other spirits near me. We drift and bump like berries boiling in a pot. Man, woman, young, old. Beach plum, blackberry, rose hip, strawberry. None of the jelly-jar labels matter anymore. Why wasn't that true in life?

Being alive was pure magic, and I've had my days of marveling at it all—the wink of sun, the first pink of spring, a caterpillar with a showy fuzz of stripes. Those everyday joys are no longer mine, but I now have a task bigger than any I had in life.

A deepwater darkness tugs at my heart. Children have always connected with spirits and vice versa—that is part of what worries me. If I was awakened, was it to keep a weather eye open for all of our young ones?

But what if I can't stop or change what I see coming?

I ring and walk and am filled with dread. But I won't hold back.

Not anymore.

Nantucket is a little island thirty miles at sea off the northeast coast of the United States, in Massachusetts. It's been famous for centuries, first for those residents who chased, caught, and survived whales and now for the dangerous game of chasing, catching, and surviving those who come to visit.

Every year between June and September, hundreds of thousands buzz in by air and sea, engines roaring and smoke billowing. A few sail in, leaving an elegant wake.

Despite the boats and planes, our island still feels remote. No bridge connects it to the mainland. It remains its soulful self, but perhaps most so during the quiet months.

A large part of its fame and glory belongs to its old homes. Mine was built in 1797, and I'm proud to say it was old when I oiled the floors, replaced a broken latch or knob, and hung dried lavender in the closets. It's even older now, and it's obviously been cherished. Only caring leaves this kind of a glow—a shine that rises from generations of hands that clean, polish, and protect.

Packed with human stories, these houses have outlived their makers and most of their owners. Like art in a museum, they are what remain.

They tell us that everyone's life matters.

Differences between the language in my day and how people now speak don't bother me. I absorb the changes, a little like your breathing air. And despite the shocking roar that brought me back, I'm learning to balance death with life, which isn't easy for most of us when alive.

Everything that's me is here, although I adapt and change form with each passing second. I'm flour being rolled into dough; a late rose dropping petals in the rain; a cat pouring itself off a chair.

From where I watch, I can see we've reached a *tipping point* on Nantucket, like the second when water flows from a pitcher. *Whoosh!* This means a critical moment when something flows in one direction and can't be stopped. Not easily.

One after another, day by day, faster and faster, our old homes are being destroyed. If people knew how much will disappear with all that old wood, they might find the strength to yell, "STOP!"

As is said at sea, all hands on deck; every last soul is needed. This is not a time for the dead to ignore the living or vice versa.

It's the kids that I especially want to catch—no, grab!—while I'm still here, because kids accept a challenge as naturally as the tide coming in. I want them to hear my bell before the *me* that's here is thrown away or ground into fragments like a shell in a storm. Before I'm only a photograph or a faded name on paper and no longer myself.

Should my house be crushed by the giant force that awakened me, I, too, will be gone.

All of us whose lives seasoned our floors and walls will disappear if that happens.

What we have to offer will vanish.

Aieee, here comes the roaring again! The way things are going around here, this could happen anytime.

Here! Take my hand. We have depths to plumb.

I like the language from the sea, don't you? In my lifetime, *plumbing the depths* meant dropping a weight on a long line over the side of a ship, in shallow waters. A person on board could measure safety that way.

You'd hit bottom and then reel in.

You'd find out how far you were from disaster.

CHAPTER 3

Lanterns at sea

Speaking of the sea and the depths, I must recount a dreadful thing that happened that last year. It haunts us all.

Late afternoon on Halloween, a Nantucket fishing boat went down with families aboard. A rogue wind came up, fog swirled in, and the instrument panel jammed. The boat, out on a special expedition, hit a shoal broadside, and all who lived were lost.

The boys and girls had each been given a child-sized hurricane lantern, a sturdy light to carry on board and use later while trick-or-treating in town. When the Coast Guard arrived after the captain's call for help, seven lamps were found bobbing miraculously on the waves, lights still bright.

I can count them now: one, two-three, four-five-six—oh, my sight blurs!—seven.

Seven amber lanterns, tossing in the foam and chop, twinkling through the gray. Impossible, of course, as those batteries don't work in salt water.

Stranger still, when rescuers bent to retrieve the bobbing lamps, they darted out of reach. Over and over, a Coast Guard crewman leaned close with a net. One light after another slipped quickly to left or right. Finally the crew gave up, and bringing the saddest and quietest of loads back to shore, they turned away from the mysteriously lit orbs. Left them dancing in the wild night. None have washed up, but there are those who claim to have seen glowing lanterns offshore at dusk.

Sometimes life is rife with sadness. In size, our island is tiny—about three miles at the widest by fourteen long—but it becomes far smaller when something dreadful happens.

Those still here, whether alive or not, share one another's agony when things go wrong.

What isn't always talked about is how. When I was alive, I learned that the line between the island's dead and those still living can blur.

At my loneliest times, I sometimes knew that I had company. I'd hear the clink of teacups and a buzz of chatting coming from the next room, or I'd be aware of little feet thumping down the stairs and then see the ivory handle on the front door rattling. I'd notice a creaking as someone walked by with quick, sure feet, or I'd hear the swish of a skirt and smell the sweet brightness of bayberry candles even when the room was dark.

I always thanked my old house.

What happens between walls lingers within them. Perhaps that's also true for disasters linked to wooden boats at sea. The waters surrounding Nantucket have more than seven hundred shipwrecks decorating the bottom. Screws and clasps and hasps and nails; broken dishes and mirrors and coins. Splintered spars and planks pickled by salty water, hidden by seaweed and fish. Bones and an occasional boot filled with rocks or sand.

The ocean has always been a complicated friend.

As are the dead.

If anything, on our island the dead work alongside those still breathing. Some always have, whether at home or at sea.

Who do you think kept those hurricane lamps lit?

Trust me. We're here.

November 1. A long year—an ache of twelve months—has passed since the boating accident.

Yesterday's annual Halloween celebrations on Main Street were subdued. Before the parade, hundreds of heads bowed for five minutes of silence to honor the dead, and even the Star Wars characters, jellyfish, pirates, and sharks never quite recovered their bounce. The anniversary of the sinking cast a gloomy shadow over this usually bubbly afternoon.

The wind dropped out early this morning, and now it's almost six p.m. and there's still not a whisper. Gulls and ducks swim in slow, darkening circles, occasionally dipping a beak to stir the calm.

Two people fish on a north shore beach. There is no one else in sight. Father and son stand in shallow water as the surface out a few yards suddenly chops and buckles.

"Gabe!" the father calls. "Looka here—what the hey, gotta be somethin' running! Hold tight to the rod, thatta way!"

A broken line of swells moves closer with a *whoosh-splash-whoosh* rhythm that sounds like people wading toward shore.

Although the sun has set, Gabe and his father can still see clearly; nothing living—man or fish—appears.

Gabe's dad, Herbie Pinkham, sucks his breath through his teeth, a quick hiss. He spins the visor on his baseball cap sideways. "Back up," he orders, reaching toward his eleven-year-old son. "Reel in!"

"But—" Gabe grips his fishing pole. "But what if I hook something?"

Alert, his dad tilts his head to one side but doesn't respond.

Soon water splashes up onto their waders. Father and son freeze, eyes following the wave. The air breathes and rustles around them. What on earth is passing by? A smooth stretch of beach at the tide line begins to crunch and wrinkle, pressed by invisible weights.

"FEET!" Gabe's dad gasps. "Looka the PRINTS! Holy mag*nees*us!"

There are no feet to be seen, but the footprints are there. Still coming, they move in a crowd.

Splish, whish, gurgle, shree—the sounds of many people wading.

Splot, shrok, spatter, crrrunch. Drops of water scatter and fly as the invisible group heads past the tide line.

Some of the feet seem to be wearing flat shoes. Others are bare. Several are unusually wide and long. Parting around Herbie's tackle box and gear, they plod slowly for the dunes, more and more of them, blurring each other's progress.

As if they're tired, Gabe thinks to himself. *Tired and cold. Young and old.* He feels a tight, tingly excitement. Just as he wonders why on earth he isn't frightened, his dad staggers sideways, his knees buckling in the icy water.

As Gabe lunges toward his father, a set of adult boot prints onshore pauses abruptly, scattering sand as if a big person had stopped in his tracks to see what was the matter.

The boy is busy and doesn't notice. He grips his dad's arm for a moment. Behind them, the water settles back to a mirror-like stillness. The sand stops moving. Whoever—or *what*ever—was passing has passed.

Father and son wade slowly toward shore. Stepping gingerly over the prints, they cross the road and begin the walk home.

Herbie Pinkham shakes so badly that the lures in his tackle box jingle and clank. Gabe has never ever seen him look frightened. *Dad is scared and I'm not*, the boy thinks with a quiet rush of delight. He glances up at his father, who looks back at him with stunned eyes. At that moment, Gabe feels at least an inch taller.

"Should never've brought you here tonight," Herbie says. "Somethin' funny in the air today. Felt it earlier. Somethin' alive, I dunno . . ."

Gabe swallows. "Do you believe in ghosts, Dad?"

At first there's no reply. Herbie is a police officer, and

Gabe knows he's seen a dead body or two. He also knows his dad likes to stick to the facts.

The boy, pleased to have his dad's attention, plows on. "*Really* believe? Like drowned ones?"

"I dunno what I believe," his dad mutters. "A lotta people have gone down offshore here, Lord knows, but . . . I've never heard of a ghost coming out of the water. Could've been a trick of the light or a rush of baitfish . . ."

Gabe reaches for the sandwich bag of homemade cookies that his mother had tucked in his pocket. He offers one to his dad, hoping to stretch the moment.

"No, thanks." Herbie Pinkham looks away.

Gabe, not hungry either, wonders where all those feet have gone and what the ghosts could see of him and his dad. He hangs the bag neatly from a bayberry bush by the side of the road.

He knows there is something out there.

~

November 4. Still no wind.

The town pier reaches into the darkening harbor this evening as Ray Ramos and his ten-year-old twins, Maria and Markus, settle down to wait, bucket and long-handled nets ready. It's low tide and they are there to catch blue crabs. The size of an adult hand, these crabs taste like lobster and are delicious in chowder. When threatened, they put up quite a fight, waving sapphire claws over their shell, pincers wide open.

Woe to the toe that steps near a blue crab in summer waters. I, Mary Chase, can still feel the shock, enough to make a person wade with eyes down from that moment on.

Come October, this species of crab heads for the deep, where they dig in for the winter months. But this week, word is out that they're close to shore, scuttling in the wrong direction.

Ray is teaching his kids to carry on the family's Portuguese, Cape Verdean traditions—such as eating all that's edible from the sea—when he isn't working in their small restaurant, which advertises home cooking with a Portuguese-plus-Caribbean flair. Maria and Markus's mom, who is from the Dominican Republic, manages the business but also makes sure the kids read lots, go to the library each Saturday, and take advantage of every offering at school. Despite having to live in one rental after another, the family is growing dreams that matter. And one day, Ray Ramos is determined, he and his wife will own a home of their own.

Like many natives—a proud name for those who are

born here—he can't afford even a smidgen of property on the island of his birth. Maria and Markus don't think about this, though—they are still young enough to believe that the island belongs to all who appreciate it.

It is Markus who spots the disturbance first.

"Pop?" he asks.

Soon all three of them can see the water surging and breaking in a long line, as if—as if what? What *is* this?

They jump to their feet, Ray pulling his children close as the churning tide gurgles and swirls beneath the planks of the pier. Small boats nearby bob gently, seemingly bumped from all sides. Seagulls perched on the tops of wooden pilings take to the air, cawing.

"Dang," Ray whispers. As the three watch, the choppy waves become water pushed by slow, solid shapes, as if people are surfacing after a hard swim, only . . . there are no people.

His daughter is the first to see the footprints. "On the beach!" she whispers, squeezing her brother's hand.

Their father's mouth falls open. First come the indentations of a man's bare feet, followed by tinier ones, feet that skip on the sand. A child? More and more prints, toes of all sizes and shapes, appear at the edge of the water, moving in an uneven gaggle up the beach and toward the grasses, the overturned rowboats, and the road into town. A few of the figures hobble as if unsure; others seem to plunge ahead with confidence and purpose, arms swinging.

Although, of course, there are no arms. No feet.

Maria's heart is pounding in her ears. Where are they going?

They don't act as if they're lost, she thinks.

"It's *them,*" Maria whispers to her brother, not knowing what she means but suddenly filled with a flush of happiness. Easily, she imagines the invisible bodies that must be attached to the feet—but why such heavy clothes, the long skirts, jackets, and all? As soon as the image enters her head—*pfft!*—it's gone.

Markus is breathless. He has a Christmas-morning feeling as he watches the footprints move slowly up the beach. *They're here, it's happening,* he thinks with relief, although he has no idea what's going on or why he's glad.

Ray Ramos, a man who has heard many stories of ghosts over the years but has never wanted to share them with his kids, plops down on the pier, his eyes huge. "What on earth," he mutters quietly.

Maria matter-of-factly scoops up a large crab and dumps it in the bucket. "Look down!" she calls out.

Her brother grabs his net and sweeps it across the bottom. "Hey," he crows. "Easy! The big ones are everywhere!"

He pulls in six, scrabbling madly over one another as he tips them into the bucket.

"They're frightened," Ray says softly, "as we should be."

Busy harvesting, his children don't hear.

Ray watches the crabs rustle over and under one another, looking for a way out. He spreads a piece of seaweed gently across his palm, as if it might speak.

CHAPTER 4

Flashes in the graveyard

Adults rarely talk about experiences they can't explain. True in my day as well. They're afraid it might make them look weak. Weak, strong, real, unreal: If only people understood how much bigger the story is.

Did I know this while alive? Sometimes I did, but a lot of the time I didn't. Everyone else was like that, too. I wish we'd kept fewer secrets.

Gabe, Maria, and Markus are all told by their parents not to let anyone hear about the inexplicable sights on the shore.

Gabe's dad, Herbie, was left speechless by the scene on the beach, although he tried to hide it from his son. On the way home, he murmured, "Well, now," several times. When Gabe said, "Dad? What *was* that?" Herbie didn't answer.

Glancing at his father, the boy rolled his eyes. *Right*, he mouthed to himself.

When they got home, Gabe babbled to his mom a quick version of what had happened. She took one look at his dad and shushed their son.

Herbie is weathered and rangy, and now that he's going silver on top, he looks more like a piece of driftwood than ever. Becky Pinkham is small and tidy, a practical person with blue eyes the color of a mussel shell. Born with a squeaky voice, Gabe is filled with questions that irritate his parents. Herbie treats open curiosity like a nose that needs a wipe, something to fix quickly while turning away. To Becky it feels dangerous, like gossip.

Over the next few days, Gabe brings up the footprints again and again, hoping to nudge his parents into talking about it. His dad, especially, does *not* want to linger on the subject.

"You listen to us now, Gabriel Pinkham," he says finally. "This island is deep and all isn't as it seems, as my grandparents used to say. They knew that and made sure that their kids and grandkids knew it, too. And we've never shared this, not wanting to startle you, but my grandma Hepsa Coffin was one who helped people to understand the—oh, the bumps and slams and unwanted visits in their old houses. She had a gift for settling restless spirits in a home, but she never told tales. Best to keep your sights on the straight and narrow. People will bother you about a story like that. Just mind your own business. Nantucket has always loved a mystery that stays that way."

Gabe's eyes glitter with hard questions as his father looks away, the topic closed. Why can't Herbie talk about this interesting stuff? Gabe wishes his dad could admit that moment of being afraid when his son wasn't! Doesn't he realize how much that would mean to Gabe? Why couldn't they share what they'd both seen? And his great-grandma, a ghost whisperer! The boy sighs.

What Gabe doesn't know is that Officer Pinkham has long felt that the dead should stay that way. He'd been frightened by his grandmother's old-fashioned work with ghosts, but was brought up not to admit it—and perhaps that is why he became a policeman, chasing facts and avoiding the unknown.

"But, Dad!" Gabe protests now, tired of his father's this-is-the-way-it-is tone. "The things that are happening—"

Herbie interrupts him. "Are *maybe* happening. Give it up."

The boy glances at a photo of his great-grandparents taken by the front door here, when both were old. Worn by sun and water, they stand elbow to elbow, as stiff as toothpicks. Herbie looks like them.

"Got it," Gabe whispers. He can't keep the disappointment out of his voice.

The three Pinkhams live not far from the Old Mill, in a modest cottage built by Herbie's grandfather. It's only four rooms, but they know how lucky they are to have it.

Gabe's mom follows her son's eyes as he looks around their home, restless with the limits that surround them. "Listen to your dad," she says gently. "I'm sure your great-grandma would agree with what he said."

Gabe wishes his *dad* would listen to *him*.

Down the road, Maria and Markus Ramos share a bedroom in the family's current rental, which they've been able to stay in for an amazing stretch of four years. Since the twins were born, the Ramoses have moved many times, like other working families on the island. This latest home is tiny; the parents sleep in the alcove next to the kitchen.

Lopsided and built all on one level, the cottage isn't far from one of the oldest graveyards, the Old North Cemetery, and the children play there in all seasons and weathers. Their parents explained that this house used to belong to the gravedigger, and joke about having one of the biggest yards on the island, one that is never empty.

"Enjoy it while you've got it!" they say. But they did caution the twins not to share what had happened on the crabbing expedition.

"Better to zip the lip on that one," Ray had told them.

When their bedroom door is closed one night not long after, Maria sits up and peers out the window.

"That them?" her brother whispers.

The two can understand each other's thoughts without saying much. Markus doesn't need to elaborate.

The moon tonight is milky, a melting scoop of vanilla ice cream. Haze puddles around the edges and it feels close, as if a kid could reach out a spoon and tilt the sky for a taste.

Markus slowly raises the storm window in their room and pokes his head outside.

As if in response, both kids see flickers of light between the scattering of stones.

"Come *on*!" he whispers, pulling clothes over his pajamas. His sister is already stuffing her nightgown into her pants. "We'll just hop out and take a peek. This isn't Halloween stuff, we're past that."

Maria grabs for her jeans and sweatshirt as her brother hunts under his bed for socks. Their parents, already asleep, don't hear.

Still as the markers that surround them, Maria and Markus spend the next half hour kneeling at the edge of the burial ground. Here and there in front of first one grave and then another, there's a quick, strange *blink*!

"Like a cell phone camera," Maria says softly to her brother.

"Or a big firefly," he adds. "Only, it's November."

Something is scattering split-second snaps of brightness, but what can it be? The lichen, the lean of the wind-scrubbed stones, a hint of lettering: Each time it happens, the glimpse seems more a flash than a sight. So fast it almost isn't. Occasionally a curl of moonlit shadow lingers between the stones, as if hunting. But when either twin points a wordless finger, the wisp slips into a greater darkness.

Only children can easily absorb what they don't understand, which makes them excellent spies. Adults, including this Crier, are always confusing what's real with what they think *should be* real.

I do my best, but I'm as guilty as the rest.

Maria knows which markers belong to children. When playing around in the graveyard during the day, she often says hello to them.

The children's stones are low, and most have a lamb

carved on the top. Maria now notices that these little markers are attracting the greatest number of flashes.

Who is out and wandering tonight? Have the footprints they'd seen coming from the water marched inland to the old burial ground to claim their children? Or even *other* children? Maria now thinks back to what she'd imagined—the long skirts and wet layers of clothing. She shivers, grateful she'd seen no faces.

Don't think about it, no! she tells herself fiercely. *Not about what the face of a person who had died in the water might look like . . . eyes filled with love for the ones left behind. Seaweed caught in hair. Teeth gleaming like wet pebbles.*

Markus glances at his sister. No need to be told what's in her mind.

The twins watch until the flickering stops. When all is still, Markus and Maria nudge each other and then stand, stamping feeling into numb feet and brushing off knees. Markus coughs.

Instantly, a bright *zing* from the middle of the burial ground catches them in a fast-as-a-minnow flicker of light.

Poof! It's gone.

They grab for each other's hands—an instant lock—and run, silent, practically flying. Behind them, twigs snap as if someone is chasing them.

Another flash.

Markus shoves Maria over the bedroom windowsill and scrambles in after her. They fall to the floor, giggling and shushing.

Neither looks back, not wanting to see.

CHAPTER 5

Beware, you who trust

November 6. Mary W. Chase again.

My feelings of darkness, of fear for our children, are founded. I quake, for I now realize that *my house* was recently sold by the old woman who kept my teapot. Over the decades, she cooked and gave away untold thousands of after-school *wonders*, soothing more kids than anyone knew. This kind spirit cared for my home perhaps as much as I did. Her name is Eliza Rebimbas, and she is now ninety-eight years old.

She met recently with a man by the name of Edwin Nold. A contractor, he is known for using the word *restore* when he means *replace*. She signed papers, not knowing what that might mean for this building so close to her heart.

Mr. Nold already has buyers waiting for Mrs. Rebimbas's house, a couple who think they want him to work on it. He speaks with them in the parking lot outside the supermarket. It's a good place to talk or eavesdrop without being noticed; people are distracted, what with shopping lists and bags. I listen.

I'd be the greatest fool to ever live or die if I wasn't terrified.

Because I know one thing for sure: As long as the settled landscape of an old house remains, we spirits, those of us whose lives were anchored in its walls and floors, who were born, gave birth, and died inside them, can stay. As can our dreams.

BUT. Rip out all of the rooms and you rip the beach from beneath the shells. You tear the poetry from the shore. You destroy what should rightfully linger. You butcher what we protect.

Gone. This Crier will vanish when her house is stripped. I, Mary W. Chase, will disappear once and for all, unable to ring my bell or shout through my horn ever again. Unable to look out for our children. Gone needlessly, and all because some who live think everything worn is trash.

Panic drives me. I have to work faster and listen even harder! I am still here, but there's not a moment to lose!

Eddy Nold is speaking. He has a slippery voice, causing some to call him Eely Eddy.

"*Sure*, I'll swing by later and we can talk," he says. "The price I gave you was a steal, as that west wall is bowed and the foundation looks like, well—like it might not stand through the week. I warned you the place needed work. And your original stairs with their old treads . . ." He breaks off and shakes his head. "Unwise. Likely to let go at any moment. Those old boards are classic but bad. So sorry. Anything that bounces and creaks won't support modern living, you know? You could fall through either floor! Renters will sue! And those uneven doorframes—tall adults could knock themselves out. You'll see, as soon as the old lady is gone . . ."

Obviously horrified, the couple nod gratefully. Once in their car, the woman buries her face in her hands.

Don't listen, whoever you are! I want to shout to her. *This is my house and it's a gem! Don't believe him!*

As Eddy climbs into his truck, a skinny man leans on the door, gray hair fluffing over the back of his sweatshirt like a squirrel's tail. His mouth moves rapidly. Opening the window, the contractor looks straight ahead, his elbow in the older man's face.

The man with the squirrelly hair is known as Robin Hood Bob—Robby Bob, for short—possibly because he used to steal from summer people who wouldn't notice a little "borrowing," as he puts it. Teak lawn furniture, a rowboat or two, bikes and tools: He "redistributed" the goods. Does he still do this? He says no, but old habits die hard.

Eddy is rude and doesn't respond to whatever Robby Bob is saying.

I study Mr. Nold at this quiet moment, as it's wise to know your enemy.

He's a fortyish man with a triangular head. Small eyes are set close on either side of a bridgeless nose. A line of mouth extends past his eyes, which seem to swivel in place, although of course that's impossible. His teeth are sharp, his ears flat. Mud-brown hair rises on the top of his head and runs clear down his neck and inside the back of his shirt. Short arms look more like pectoral fins than anything useful, which is odd in a person who does physical labor.

His voice is perhaps his greatest weapon. He uses the word *sure* like salt on fries, and makes it sound just as good. He's the first at the sale of every old house that's still an antique, especially in my neighborhood, an area in town with a bunch of old buildings.

I've been catching up on the rules. There are now strict ones on Nantucket about not disturbing the outside of an old structure, but nothing protects the inside. Lately, people have been buying our old houses and throwing away everything inside, just because it's been around forever. That, and the rooms are small and ceilings low. The new owners might leave a few of the original boards buried beneath fresh shingles or hidden under drywall, in order to later claim the structure is from 1803 or perhaps even 1745. When the job is done, all appears—and is!—new, despite a plaque on the building claiming it's old. Inside, you could be anywhere—Florida, San Francisco, Phoenix. Such interiors feel like anywhere and nowhere at the same time.

Eddy is one of those contractors. He is proud of the name Nold Builders. *All the comforts of NEW inside the OLD* promises a banner on the side of his truck. *Nold, not mold!* is lettered neatly across the back.

Insisting that he does what he does for the good of the people he works for or buys from, he always has a smear of dirt somewhere on his body, as if wanting to give the message that he's too busy to stay clean. He volunteers at the Nantucket Children's Club, and sometimes at the food pantry. Oddly, Eddy is liked at both places. An import from the mainland when the economy took a dip, he's been on the island for only a few years but always seems to know where to be and when, especially if an old house like mine comes up for sale.

Eliza Rebimbas still has her wits about her. Decades ago, she and her husband, Tony, were famous for their intricate lightship baskets, a tightly woven rattan basket of a purse with a smooth wooden base and scrimshaw on the lid. This type of basketmaking was exacting work, an old craft done well only by a few.

Eliza's husband has passed, her only daughter and then granddaughter have both died, and her grandson, his wife, and *their* two children—she didn't see much of them, but was happy they were still on-island—were swept away in last year's boating accident.

This dreadful event left her without living family, a shocking turn of events, but she continues to bake her wonders for the schoolchildren. She is known in the community as Grandma Rebimbas.

Eddy Nold knocked on her door months ago and returned to visit several times. After complimenting her on her generosity with kids, he suggested that were she to sell her home to him, she could then give the proceeds to the Children's Club. He assured her that he worshipped the old and "Nantuckety," after oohing and aahing over her house and calling it a find. He talked about how an old house deserves to be restored, like an old piece of art.

Someone should have recorded Eddy's words.

"Do we destroy a Leonardo da Vinci painting simply because it needs to be repaired or the frame is beat up?" he asked Mrs. Rebimbas. "Of course not!"

She believed him.

A nearby neighbor, Lydia Lyon, had a similar experience. Lydia was also old and without living family; she and Eliza had shared much of their lives over the back fence that divided their properties—sicknesses, weddings, soups, and extras of all kinds. If one of them had too many fresh vegetables, she'd send some "over the fence" with one of the neighborhood kids, who might then return with a basket of berries or a pot of stew. Lydia Lyon also sold her home to Nold Builders, believing this would save it.

Eely Eddy had promised both Mrs. Lyon and Mrs. Rebimbas that they could stay in their homes until ready to leave. The elderly women were grateful.

Last week, Mrs. Lyon died peacefully in her sleep, and it became clear that interior demolition would begin immediately on her house. Nold trucks and backhoes rolled past the Rebimbas home, and the walls trembled.

Shocked, saddened, and frightened, Eliza had a fall the next day. A broken hip and cracked elbow sent her to the hospital shortly after . . . and from there straight to the island's nursing home.

That, I believe, is when I was startled awake.

The house needed me.

Mrs. Rebimbas hears today that Eddy Nold is grumbling to people around town that her place—meaning mine, too!—is unsound.

It isn't.

The only unsound thing here is Eely Eddy's grasp of the truth. He said the same thing about Lydia Lyon's house.

Eliza wishes she'd never heard the news.

Our house is worn, yes, the floors uphill and down, but the structure is solid as can be. One of a kind. Built by a shipwright—that is, a skilled carpenter who built boats—over two hundred years ago. Mended, tended, and lived in by generation after generation of working people. "A one-of-a-kind monument to the work of hands"—that's how Eliza liked to describe her home. *Our* home.

Eliza's baskets hang from the rafters, and my old copper pots shine on the walls. Needlework samplers and a few paintings keep company with braided rugs. Plates and teacups were brought from China by some of my husband's whaling relatives. The place was once home to Benjamin Franklin's great-niece, who was a Folger and the first wife in the house; it's belonged to house and ship carpenters, a mason, a blacksmith, even a Civil War veteran—my husband, Daniel. Fifteen babies have been born in the house, and at least a dozen people have died in it.

This structure will welcome any who respect its age.

"Like an old picnic basket or chair," Eliza explained to Eddy Nold, who pretended to agree.

"Nothing like an angle that's settled," she added, talking about everything in life.

And now her house is quiet, with no smells of fried dough or an evening fire, and her neighbor's old home is under attack.

She hears the news from a nurse.

"Much of Mrs. Lyon's place is gone. And I know those Nold Builders. What they do to a house makes it look like new," the woman reports. Perhaps she doesn't realize that Eliza also sold her home to Eely Eddy. "Something from a real estate ad," the nurse chats on, straightening sheets. "Never know that an old house was once inside those walls. Just a brand-spanking, whoop-de-do copy.

"I drove by another one of his 'projects' last night—you know he always does a few at the same time. Didn't recognize a thing. Scooped out like a fish or a melon. Shutters gone, all new windows, a chandelier in the front parlor where the owners used to have an old ship's lantern, the brass always twinkling. Nold added those way-too-bright ceiling lights, the kind that make you squint, and shiny paint on the front clapboards. Can see your reflection, driving by. Ah, me." She pauses, seeing Eliza's face.

"He's making a fancy ballroom version of our world, like in a Hollywood movie."

Eliza's eyes close and a tear rolls down one cheek.

"Did I upset you, dear?" the nurse asks. "I'm sorry, how thoughtless of me."

"Remember," Eliza whispers to all who stop to greet her after that, "to join hands."

The staff smile, looking touched but puzzled. Several give her hand a squeeze.

It's easy to forget that a very old Nantucketer is a series of layers, like an oyster shell, with a young person inside.

A child with a pearl for a heart and a knowing mind.

I hear her. I wish I could tell her that Mary W. Chase is here. And awake. That strange events are happening on the shore, at dusk. That she isn't alone.

I wish I could warn her that I don't know how to stop the rumbling. Shaken by the nurse's words, I leave Eliza's bedside to check on our home. It is reassuringly dark and still. I hurry around the corner to look at Mrs. Lyon's place.

No! I hear a towering wave of ghostly voices—people calling out, babies crying. Chaos. Wreckage. If I wasn't already dead, I'm sure this moment would have killed me.

CHAPTER 6
Witness

Before I share the horrors of what I've just witnessed, let's pause.

Walk by me for a moment.

For over a week now, not a breath of air has lifted a leaf, offering no way to explain the unseen visitors from the water. The wind, after all, can make a person feel strange things. A shirt huffing on a clothesline or a branch tossing and bobbing can fill the imagination. But no movement at all . . .

It's said that the anniversary of a tragedy can deepen its effect. One year after the fishing boat went down, it took the wind with it, as if to leave us all listening.

But listening for what? Or whom?

Surely not Eddy and his earthmoving machines.

Folks here are still whispering to one another about the timing of the boat accident. Halloween, or All Hallows' Eve, is an ancient celebration day, one that reaches back before Christianity to the Romans and the Celts. To the people who lived across Europe—especially England and Ireland—on islands similar to Nantucket in size and climate, it was a day to mark the end of summer and the beginning of the darker part of the year.

The Celtic word for this day of transition is *Samhain*, pronounced *sah-win*. Across Northern Europe, it was often about ringing bells to wake and welcome the dead, then inviting them back home for a visit and offering them food such as apples, nuts, and soul cakes. A treat and some tenderness. Lighting candles so they could see their way.

Hallowing and *hollowing*: funny how close the words are. They mean such different things, one filling and one emptying. I'd like it if the island's old homes were all hallowed and not hollowed.

I wouldn't have to worry.

When I was a girl, many brought a lantern and a home-baked sweet to the graves of their loved ones. It wasn't unusual to see lights twinkling between the stones on October 31. In the Quaker cemetery, the rolling field without many markers, you could always see a lantern here and there, glimmering through the grasses.

I'm thinking of everyday islanders like me, not the famous or rich ones. I'm talking about those who chopped their own wood, mended fishing nets, tended their vegetables, saved the rainwater that ran off the roof, scrubbed until their knuckles were raw, sewed everything they wore, salted and pickled food, kept an eye on one another's kids, and went out on handcrafted boats. Perhaps this is a part of what's gotten us off balance.

Caused us to tip.

Life on the island revolves around the wind and the ocean. After all, everyone here both works and relaxes on or near the water, and the boats won't run if the weather gets bad.

We call that a "no-boat day." Those who belong to the island refer to the ferry as *the boat.* Say anything else and people will know you don't belong. Even the big ferries, the ones that carry giant trucks and all the passenger cars, are simply *boats.*

The island has been buffeted for centuries by hurricanes and countless nor'easters. It's not much bigger than a giant's sand castle, and some would say not much more solid. Spray can land on windows two miles from the beach.

The south side bravely faces the Atlantic Ocean and South America, and there is no other land between the easternmost sand dunes and Portugal. Every winter the beaches change shape as the sand whirls, and often a house on the edge slides in, its window curtains flapping sadly at the march of waves. Have you ever seen a home consumed by the ocean, roof shingles and chimney vanishing under the breakers, spice jars and bright pillows floating out through broken panes? It's a violent sight, and during such a storm it's hard to remember calm.

Which brings us back to this November. Has there *ever* been a month, in any season, when the wind around Nantucket Island stopped blowing?

The eleventh month of the year on this tiny piece of land is often a time of settling. Sit-ting, set-ting, set-tling—I like that, don't you? Sounds like a generous skirt being lowered onto a cane chair seat. A crunch and a crackle, followed by a sigh.

November is our thinking month—a time of crisp, bright moons and of liquid mockingbirds in the tallest trees. The tourists are now gone and the hurricanes have passed. Skies can be cool and gentle as the inside of a clamshell, a powdery wash of cream drifting toward lavender. There is the mournful *whooo-hooo* of the old ferry whistle, the many church bells speaking in turn, seagulls coasting overhead, and then the wind whisking and sifting through the falling leaves. Mostly, though, there are deep pools of silence, a silence that isn't silent to us all.

It's the *ohhh*-sound of a bedroom door opening in a sleeping house.

The catlike purr of an underwater current pulling over sand.

Wish, whishhhh . . .

Perhaps it's the whisper of what's possible. Shhh, listen! Is that an echo inside my horn, or is it the sound of conversation between the living and the dead?

This Crier quakes for herself and for others. When our homes are hollowed out, it's not just the work of many hands over many years that will vanish.

We who now surround the living, unseen but not unfelt, will not be able to chime in. Once that happens, there is no bringing us back.

Around here, the new is a shadow of the old.

~

All remains eerily still today. Every movement seems bigger than it is and each sound louder.

What I just saw happen to Lydia Lyon's house is hard to share. Gathering courage, I hug my horn and bell to my heart.

The house, nestled into a street laid out in the early

1700s, was lived in for centuries, like mine. Repairs had kept it happy. Leaks and rot were fixed when found and cracks sealed. The structure boasted some of the most beautiful pine floorboards in town, honey-colored planks more than two feet wide.

This house was far from dead.

What happened next still feels like now: I hear screams as joists are ripped apart. Rafters and corner posts shiver in their sudden nudity. Thick wood trembles and sobs. No avoiding the truth: After centuries of comfort behind plastered walls, *whoosh*! The innards of this old house are dying in the cool, bright air.

I am a witness. And while I can't see the faces of all who'd been at rest inside that old structure, I can hear their voices and feel their startled breathing on my cheek, can sense them circling and know their hands are groping for help.

I reach back, hoping to connect, but touch only air. Devastated, I imagine the death of my own home. Whose cries will go unanswered then?

At that darkest of moments, I hear children. A boy and a girl! It's the same two I saw through my window when I was first awakened by the roaring: Gabe, from the beach, and that girl with the tangled hair. Their eyes are bright with horror.

Hearing that Mrs. Lyon had died and that Grandma Rebimbas might want cheering up, they had stopped at her house after school. Her front door was locked, and scary noises came from the property nearby. They'd hurried into her backyard, school backpacks bouncing, to look.

And here we are. They do not see me, but I am grateful for their company.

The boy, biting his lip, turns pale as a clam. He stares at the area around the fireplace, in the heart of Lydia Lyon's old house. Eyes darting, he studies the second floor, then the first. A board crashes, popping nails, and the boy takes a quick step toward the house as if to interfere. He can't, of course. The rear wall of the building falls, and a backhoe rips through an inside room. The tinkle of breaking glass, the dust of centuries-old plaster, the crack and groan of wood: It's an ugly scene. The girl's fists are clenched and she speaks fast, spinning away to brush off tears she doesn't want him to see.

I am startled by the girl, feeling we are somehow connected. Her name is Phee, like the start of the word *fierce*. I reach out to comfort her, but she moves suddenly, stamping her foot. We do not touch.

The boy and the girl are now waving their arms and shouting at the workers on the property. They step bravely toward the demolition fencing, but no one seems to care.

"Heyyyy!" I hear Phee's voice warbling over the noise.

"Hey, *you* in there!" Gabe shouts. "Please, mister!" The man in the backhoe looks right at the kids but doesn't react.

I hate it when adults treat the young as if they aren't even there.

I look back toward the house and gaze up at a giant but healthy elm in the yard, one filled with birds each morning and witness to more than two centuries of living. A monstrous machine has arrived, and now the three of us watch it saw, grind, and chip the life out of that proud tree. Branches still humming with green are tossed in a pile. A buzz saw hacks yards of roots from the soil.

Shocking, I tell you! Destroying one of these elms is like killing a living piece of the island, one that offers dignity and grace to us all. The owners wanted *more sun* on their porch. More sun! And here they are, out in the middle of the ocean on a sandbar.

There are consequences, of that I am sure. Such crimes, the brutal gutting of a house or the needless taking of an ancient tree, surely awaken all who are gone but still here.

For longer than the girl, the boy studies the wreckage of the house and yard. Now she touches his arm and they turn away. I follow the children's gloom as they head for Phee's home. I feel their mood in the slump of young shoulders and the determined shuffle of sneakers through leaves.

Wait! My heart—unseen, but still here!—is thudding. The three of us are far from alone.

The air is filled with life but does not move. Clouds and ocean and land are rolling, like crumbs on God's knee. Colors drift. Now a darkening cobalt sky frames the gleam of low tide, and sand glitters and flows beneath a rising moon.

The late light is ours! They're back. Many others. I can't see them, but I can *feel* them.

And like the worn cobblestones in our streets, the rumpled brick sidewalks and the sinewy arms of elms, we belong.

I wonder how many of us are here and whether we will matter. I think of the tear rolling down Eliza's cheek, and our poor, dear house, so close to that dreadful scene. My teapot, peering anxiously out the kitchen window.

I ring! I blow! "I'm here!" I shout. "HERE! HERE! HERE!"

But no one replies.

The boy and girl walk on. Oh, why can't they hear me?

CHAPTER 7

A chat, a game, a lure

"Gabe?" Phee's head pops up.

The two are passing through narrow streets in the oldest part of town, where many houses stand empty in the off-season. She stops abruptly and sits down on some steps.

Silence.

"GABE. What happened back there?" The boy joins her. It is then that Phee sees her old friend's eyes are swimming with tears. "Oh. Sorry. I know this stinks."

Gabe shakes his head. "I'm just so *mad*," he says slowly. "And I know my parents won't want me to talk about any of this."

"But talking to *me* doesn't count," Phee reminds him. Both have odd voices that stand out in a group, which first made them notice each other in school—Gabe's sounds like bicycle brakes that need oil and Phee's is a low croak.

Another reason they've been friends for so long is that their families are opposites. Phee lives alone with her grandfather, Absalom Folger, on Main Street. Everyone calls him Sal and he calls his granddaughter Fee-fi-fo Phee because of her giant-sized determination. Their home is often messy and there are few rules, like when to go to bed or what and how to eat. No one bothers about homework or whether you've gotten the dirt off your shoes. Nor does anyone worry if you're late or haven't left a note.

Gabe's place, on the other hand, is strict and quiet. Not much is said and lots can't be talked about, as if messy ideas aren't polite. Everything happens on schedule. To Phee, this is exotic and puzzling. For Gabe, it's frustrating and sometimes lonely.

Visiting each other feels good to both. Phee has always enjoyed the orderly atmosphere at Gabe's, and his dad's way of watching over them as if they might vanish, like soap bubbles or water boiling in the bottom of a pan. She also loves his mom's gooey chocolate cookies.

Phee and Gabe study each other's faces for a moment.

"Well? What is it?" Phee says, unable to be patient for another second.

"There's stuff I haven't told you, because my parents were so worried about it. You know, well, *spirit* stuff. I've been sitting on it for days."

First, Gabe fills her in on what he and his dad saw on the beach. Then he tells his friend about his great-grandma Hepsa Coffin. Phee's eyes are wide but she only nods, biting her lip. She knows that interrupting a Pinkham is dangerous to any story—it could mean the end of it.

"And just now, at the house site," Gabe mutters, "I saw some kids. Through that hole at the back. A boy wearing a straw hat stood on the second floor, and when the board under him fell, he jumped. Landed down below, by the fireplace. And then nails flew through the air, plus a shower of broken things, and he didn't seem to notice. Like they flew right through him, and the hat stayed on."

Phee's mouth is now open.

"On the first floor, he disappeared and then popped out again, pulling a girl who clutched a cloth doll, one of those old-fashioned ones with a china head and feet. The two kids held hands and rushed toward the front door. Then the boy stopped just inside, looked around, and gestured to me. *Me!* All frantic. Like it was an emergency."

Gabe pauses and Phee, desperate for him to continue, bobs her head up and down like one of those puppies stuck to the dashboard in a car. Her friend goes on. "The boy went like *this* with one hand, as if to say, *Hurry up, you!* Then the two of them stepped into a crowd of adults standing just inside the front door, people with old stuff on. Long skirts. Bonnets. Foul-weather gear like rain slickers. Some were solid, some just outlines. One of them had a flat basket, another an oar. It didn't seem like anyone but the boy noticed me. Then *bam!* Another board fell from the second floor and thick dust puffed everywhere. When it cleared, all those people were gone."

"Wow. That's *it*," Phee says softly. "You're one of *them*."

"I am NOT!" Gabe says indignantly. "What are you talking about?"

"Like your great-grandma. You have a talent for seeing ghosts! My grandpa Sal says it runs in families. Some are born with it, some aren't. And if you live on a place like this island, with lots of old buildings, well . . ." Phee sounds far too cheerful.

"I don't want to be able to do that!" Gabe moans. "I'd have to hide it from my parents. They'd say I couldn't go *anywhere* on my own if the dead are trying to make friends. I hate all of this."

"Gabriel Pinkham," Phee replies in her bossiest voice. "This is cool."

"I feel sick," Gabe says, then reties both of his sneakers, his chin resting on first one knee and then the other. "Like I might barf. How can *I* help those kids? By stopping the house-wrecking? Me? A kid?"

"*We*," Phee corrects.

"Okay, *we*." Gabe looks down the street. "*We*. But what if those spirits are, well, depending on us? And we can't help?"

"Hmm." His friend squints, kicking at a pebble by her foot. "Seemed more like they wanted you to stop asking questions and start *doing*."

"You sound like my dad. And since he saw the steps on the beach, too, but has decided he didn't . . . nah. He'll do his best not to believe. Everything in his world has to fit with what the police say is real." Gabe's mouth turns down.

"I think your dad would do anything for you," Phee says gently. "But he probably thinks the smartest thing to do is nothing."

"Yeah," Gabe says, the word heavy. "Nothing."

"But we know it isn't," Phee says. "That boy wants your help. And you saw them all waiting. Mrs. Lyon's place must have been their home first."

"ARGHHH," Gabe mutters. "So the only thing to do

is to stop this house-gutting—but if someone on Nantucket owns an old house, they can *legally* do whatever they want to the inside. But this is so cruel, with spirits involved, and it's wrong. WRONG."

"Why do you say 'spirits'?" Phee asks.

"Sounds less scary than 'ghosts.'"

Phee looks around at the quiet street. "Do you think your dad could talk to Mr. Nold about what he's up to? Like, persuade him that it's awful to rip apart these old houses?"

Gabe turns away, his expression oddly like one of Herbie's. "Unlikely."

"*Unlikely* means *possible,*" Phee says brusquely. She hops to her feet, takes a few determined steps, then stops when she realizes Gabe isn't next to her. "Come on, you slowpoke—there's not a moment to waste. Spirits, ghosts—it doesn't matter what you call 'em. Either way, this is an emergency. Let's see what the Gang has to say, instead of heading home to my place."

As Gabe adjusts his backpack, his face brightens. "Hey! What if this is something meant for kids, and kids only—and maybe that's why I saw them? That day my dad and I saw the footprints on the beach, he was pretty shaken up, but I had this strange bubbly feeling, like—well, like I was *glad* the spirits were there. I kind of felt like I could rescue my dad, if needed. Like I recognized something he didn't. And I hung some cookies on a bush for whoever belonged to the footprints, in case anyone was hungry."

Phee grins at her friend. "Good move," she says. "Onward."

As the Crier, I'm amazed how *little* adults know about how *much* kids think.

I feel a bit dizzy with that idea. Being an adult most recently, that is.

Kids live in a far more interesting world than their parents do, in part because they are always spying. Spying and living in the present.

And here's a secret: When you're really in the present, I believe you're most in the past, because it never actually went away. It's what makes us all people and not horseshoe crabs or stones. Many who live think the past isn't here, but those of us who've died know better.

Half an hour later, the kids in the Old North Gang are sitting in a circle among the stones in the Old North Cemetery, halfway between Phee's and Gabe's homes. Friends for years now, the Gang consists of Gabe and Phee, Maria and Markus, and three other kids—Paul,

Cyrus, and Maddie Coffin. The last three live in a one-story cottage owned by their grandmother, one bordering the burial ground.

Ranging in age from six to eleven, each one of the kids in the Gang has seen things they can't explain. They are open with one another. Gabe has just told the rest of the Gang what he shared with Phee on the steps, with a warning not to repeat his story; Maria and Markus have told the others about the invisible shapes wading out of the water and then the lights that chased them from the graveyard. The Coffin kids have the greatest backlog of stories, being the ones who live right next to hundreds of graves. They've seen a tiny girl who calls herself Mary Abby and sometimes appears in a white dress, wanting to play; they've seen a woman in a long skirt and hat who always sits quietly by a cluster of slate gravestones, painting a picture; they've seen a man with a beard and a woman with a long braid who like to stroll arm in arm, but then vanish into nothing if you try to get too close.

When Gabe now fills them in on the boy signaling frantically for help and the little girl by his side, eyes are big.

"Sounds desperate," Cyrus says.

"Poor kids." Maria nods. "Losing their home."

"I'd bring my doll, too," Maddie chirps.

They decide that one adult in particular might be able to help in this crisis, and that's because he's lived through more ups and downs in his lifetime than most. That person is Sal Folger, Phee's grandfather.

Before the kids leave the graveyard, I need to share a bit more about this Coffin family and a certain game played by the Gang.

It's a game that lures ghosts.

Paul, Cyrus, and Maddie Coffin have two living parents, but both work on an offshore fishing trawler and are sometimes gone for weeks. When they're home, this mom and dad often do too much "celebratin'," as their grandma Sue calls it. The kids are just as happy to be living with her.

The three feel lucky that their grandma's cottage is next to an unfenced graveyard; there are no cars, just an occasional rabbit or a curious deer. The house is cramped—"the size of a polite sneeze," their grandma says fondly—and sometimes one kid or another takes a game, a book, or a snack and leans against a headstone to do homework outside or simply be alone. During the hot months, the kids have sometimes crept in among the stones at night to find a breeze under the stars and look for ghosts. The burial ground is never a sad place for them. Rather, it feels as if they're in a friendly gathering spot, as their grandma is related to most of the people buried nearby. Of course, this means that they are, too.

"You kids belong," Grandma Sue reminds them comfortably. "Coffins, Husseys, Bartletts, Gardners, Folgers. Family. Nothing out there will ever hurt you. Just folks who went to sea, caught whales, cooked everything to the bone, and made do."

The Ramos and Coffin kids are neighbors and spend lots of time together. Gabe and Phee, both "only" kids, like to stop by after school, as they did today. The Old North Gang's favorite game is one taught to them by Grandma Sue, who calls it Ghost Gam.

The word *gam* comes from life at sea. When two whaling ships ran across each other in one of the oceans and the captains wanted to talk, one was rowed to the other ship and they got together for a gam.

Nantucket language is packed with those nautical terms—you can't get away from them. "Once at sea, never off it," we islanders say.

Here's how Ghost Gam works: One kid—called the Captain—quietly picks a name from the children's markers in the graveyard, of which there are many. He or she then writes down the chosen name, stuffs it in a pocket, and wanders around silently repeating the dead child's name until a clear picture of something comes to mind, something that feels like a *surprise.* The Captain then adds this by the name. It might be a family of china animals or a jack-in-the-box, a live puppy, a painted toy boat, or a rocking horse.

In the Captain's pocket, a scrap of paper might say:

Little Emmy & baby chick

or

James Hussey & spinning top

The others then ask twenty questions about this thing that came to mind, such as: Does it move? Ever breathe? Is it a pet? Is it made of wood? Was it carved?

The Gang is good at this game and almost always guess right. Next, they all gather around that headstone and leave the piece of paper next to the grave, tucked under a heavy stone or shell from Grandma Sue's beach-combing pile. They chant, "Here you are, and so are we. Here's your gift, so please be free."

When the Gam is over, one of the kids calls out,

"Grandma Su-u-ue!" in a teasing singsongy voice. Sue Coffin opens her kitchen door and sings back, "WHO wins the WON-DER?" and all the kids feel happy and excited because although there's really no winner or loser, she rolls *wonder* off her tongue as if it's as sweet and rare as a winter goldfinch.

And what a wonder it is—a heavenly circle of fried dough dipped in either chocolate, maple syrup, or a mix of sugar and cinnamon. Everyone gets one.

Grandma Sue loves this game, as she feels the children buried nearby could always use a toy and some play rather than a sad glance. As the Gang piles into her kitchen and reaches for the wonders, she always says the same thing: "Here's to all, so bite the lure!"

A lure, of course, is nothing unusual to people living on a small island. Comparing a treat to a fishhook doesn't trouble either this grandma or the group of kids.

As in many families run by a grandparent, the three Coffin children fit like puzzle pieces. Paul, never shy, is eleven and pretends always to know which way the wind is blowing, which usually works. People think he does even when he doesn't. Cyrus, nine, is the one who keeps an eye or ear out for trouble, especially during this silent month when thoughts are extra loud. Grandma Sue says he's lucky to be "the Coffin with deep waters," which makes him feel special. Maddie is six, the baby in the family, and happily notices and announces things the other two miss. She doesn't yet write well enough to be a Captain in Ghost Gam, but she can partner with one of the older kids.

After the brief Gang meeting in the cemetery that afternoon, Paul calls out, "Grandma Su-u-ue! Going to Phee's place for a bit," and his grandmother pops her head out the kitchen window.

"Already?" She frowns. "Gam done, or aren't you kids playing today?"

Maddie waves back. "Gotta see—" she squeaks, then stops as the others nudge her.

Grandma Sue scans their faces. "Well, okay. Hold on to your sister." Grandma Sue nods to Paul and Cyrus.

As she turns away from the window, she mutters, "I'll keep those wonders warm . . ."

Phee's grandfather hears the shuffle-bump of many feet on the stairs before he sees the kids.

As he listens to the news about Mrs. Rebimbas's empty house and the deadly treatment of Lydia Lyon's place next door, his eyes darken with anger. Gabe then describes the boy who signaled for help, the little girl clutching the doll, and the crowd by the front door.

Sal nods grimly. "You're right—those folks need us. Make yourselves at home till I get back," he says. "Gotta check in with someone."

"But not my dad! He hates this stuff and doesn't want me talking about it," Gabe blurts. "Please don't!"

"Not your dad," Sal repeats. He pauses. "But don't ever underestimate a parent," he says slowly. "Or grandparent," he adds with a wink as the door closes.

~

Minutes later, after walking rapidly past Mrs. Rebimbas's empty house and standing by the stripped-down wreckage that was once Lydia Lyon's proud home, Sal sits by Eliza Rebimbas's bed in the island nursing home.

She raises one hand. "Must stop it," she murmurs. Still as can be, she listens to all Sal has to say.

A nurse marches in and interrupts. "Pills, Mrs. R.! Time for your nighty-night pain meds!"

Mrs. Rebimbas takes the medicine, closing her eyes in resignation. When the nurse is gone, Eliza gazes directly at Sal, her blue eyes as sharp and kind as ever.

"I'll do my best," Sal promises, looking at his hands. "As will the children."

"Yes, the children . . ." Mrs. Rebimbas looks out the window. "Children and ghosts. Like sugar with cinnamon."

Her eyes slide shut and Sal sits for a moment longer, remembering what had happened to him at her house when he was a boy.

The dead had stepped in and straightened him out.

CHAPTER 8

Who will rescue us?

Let's talk about ghosts. Spirits. Souls. Poltergeists.

This Crier doesn't know exactly who's out there.

Thousands of people have lived over the centuries on this tiny island: If we were all present at the same time, it would be a nightmare.

I mean it. We Nantucketers have always valued our privacy.

Every island resident has heard stories of the dead crossing paths with the living. This has gone on for longer than I can remember, but some aren't sure what to think or say about this stuff. I mean, whether or not to believe in a spirit that seems to interact. Well, here's the truth: All folks change their tune once they've had an experience of their own.

Sometimes it's seeing a figure, or even a number of figures; other times, there are bumps, thumps, footsteps, latched doors that open. Objects are moved. Snatched. Dropped. Mostly the experience is comforting, as the sounds in my house were. Occasionally a visit is threatening.

Perhaps it's a scary face, a patch of freezing air, or a suffocating pressure pinning a person to the bed at night.

Anger and urgency don't evaporate with death, you know. Some souls remain disturbed, and no doubt have good reason for making a fuss.

Others are surprised. Working. Busy, like me.

Most ghost stories do center on an old house. A place like Eliza Rebimbas's and mine, at least if Eddy Nold doesn't get to it.

Ohhh, perish the thought! If my house is gone and I am, too, who will ring and hoot?

"OHHHHHH! Does anyone hear me? HELP us!" My voice bleeds across a quiet sunset, a streak of darkness against the orange light. People watching shudder. Grandma Sue closes her kitchen window; Eliza Rebimbas rests her eyes and thinks of happier times.

I work at being louder. *"OHHHHH, who will rescue us?"*

As the sun drops below the waves, all is still.

~

It's said that the ghosts of those who were here before modern times are tougher than recent spirits, perhaps because death was always around the corner.

Despite my moment of desperation, I feel hope. I'm surrounded by far greater strengths than my own, and I don't mean the Eddy Nolds of the world. I'm thinking of those who went to sea in the days before engines and radar and satellites. Those who remained on this island for centuries, despite illness and hardship.

Although not all may have reached out while alive, they are now freer.

Most of us who come back are here for two reasons. One, our home is still intact, the wood and plaster saturated with our everyday doings. We drift in and out, the way I used to do. Two, we are needed.

Maybe it's an invitation that few souls can resist, an urge that becomes stronger after death, as if once we've stopped breathing, we're better at helping others. Now we're able to offer what was given to us when *we* were still flesh and blood, although we might not have been aware at the time of the gift.

Perhaps we spirits are like folded towels on a kitchen shelf. Out we come—snap! flap!—at the right moment. To dry tears. To mop up spills. To soothe.

To be present.

I'm back with a willing hand.

I have two. Here—hold tight.

CHAPTER 9

Empty space that isn't

While Sal returns from his visit with Mrs. Rebimbas, the Gang fishes for ideas around the woodstove in Phee's warm kitchen.

Life at the Folger house wasn't always this cozy. Sal and Phee were thrown together by a storm.

Phoebe Folger Antoine—pronounced *Fee-bee Fol-jer An-twon*—appeared eleven years ago on an old sailboat in Nantucket Harbor. Born early and small, she refused to give up despite complications, rousing the entire harbor with her shrieks. She has always been headstrong. Her mom, Sal's daughter, Flossie, is now away and her dad, Jules Antoine, has returned to Haiti, where he's from. Things didn't exactly work out between him and her mom; they made some "bad choices," as a school counselor once put it. Phee remembers thunderous fights, the boat rocking wildly as her parents pushed each other and threw heavy things against the walls, once shattering a porthole.

At age five, she awoke alone on the boat one windy night. Curled up in her bunk down below, stuffed animals held tight, she listened as the wood creaked and moaned. Water began to trickle through the cracks, something that wasn't supposed to happen. Soon her pillow was wet. She called to her parents, but both were ashore working. This wasn't unusual; she knew they were often gone while she slept.

Suddenly a deep voice boomed, "Permission to come abooooard!" and unfamiliar boots thumped across the deck. A head peered down through the hatch. A member of the Coast Guard draped a jacket over her pajamas and brought her to the police station in town, where her grandfather Sal picked her up.

A ferocious nor'easter blew up overnight, swamping the boat, which needed repairs. Phee has lived with her grandfather from that moment on. His home is now hers, and vice versa.

Her mother, Flossie Folger, left soon after for a California university where she's worked for years on a degree in the preservation of historic buildings. *Steering the past into the future*, as Sal explains it. He says that, as a kid, she always loved listening to stories about their old family home, and believed that secrets were hidden in the cracks and knotholes. Good with a hammer and nails, she spoke to and patted the walls. Sal says she's always had a soft spot for Nantucket's weathered houses, and that learning how best to protect them is the perfect career for her.

Sal is a can-do guy. Not everyone in the community knows that, as he keeps to himself. He and Phee talk lots, but he and the rest of the world talk little. As sometimes happens if you jump a generation, Sal and his young granddaughter understand each other without even trying.

Phee does still miss things about her mom: Flossie's cheerful humming and lemony scent; the sight of a crescent of stars always clipped in her hair; a jingly tangle of arm bracelets; and the made-up stories, ones starring friendly sharks, hurricanes that became cozy hammocks, a cool sun and a warm moon that loved each other. Phee and her mother played a simple game: If Flossie hadn't seen Phee for a few hours, she would ask, "Where's my big girl?" and try to look as if she didn't recognize her daughter. Phee would then shout, "Here! I'm *right here*!" and Flossie would shriek and grab her for a hug.

Of course, there were the bad times when her parents were angry at each other, but Phee remembers that less well.

Her mom and Sal have been writing for all these years.

Phee adds her news to the bottom of Sal's letters. They haven't heard from Flossie for months now, but Sal isn't worried. He says the end of a degree is probably the hardest part, and that is why she's been silent.

Phee's dad left no address, but Phee will try to find him when she's older. A house painter, Jules always smelled delicious, like salt plus turpentine. She remembers he had broad, cozy shoulders and taught her a game played on the deck of their houseboat with chicken bones, dried beans, and scallop shells.

Meanwhile, she's happy in town with Sal. More than happy.

They make an odd pair. Sal is tall and faded; Phee, short and vivid.

She likes her grandfather's pirate-y looks. He comes complete with a sock hat, no matter what the season, a broken front tooth, chin stubble, and one lazy eye. Difficult teeth run in the family; Phee has uneven chompers that boast a whistling gap in front, and pointy incisors give her a slightly dangerous grin.

She likes to comb her long black hair until it bounces and shines. Her eyebrows can wander away from each other but rush together when she's angry. If she wants to be fancy, she puts on invisible eye shadow with a smooth nubbin of shell, and powders her nose with a leaf.

Phee's taught her grandfather how to play the Jamaican chicken-bone-and-beans game. Sal teaches his granddaughter never to feel sorry for herself, no matter what, and never to stop thinking about how to repair and recycle the broken things in life. Being an islander, he tells her, means being a problem solver.

The Folger house has been in the family since it was built in 1783. It doesn't exactly fit in with its neighbors anymore—the place buckles and leans, and the yard is a maze of wooden barrels and sea chests bound with iron, a blacksmith anvil surrounded by tools, old carriage wheels, a tangle of anchors, weeds as tall as Phee, and neat stacks of fireplace mantels and brick.

Things other people might need or want one day.

Sal and Phee have noticed that some of their off-island neighbors have gotten unfriendly over the last year or so. Gathering on the sidewalk in front, they talk and gesture but without so much as a nod to Sal if he happens to walk by. Eddy Nold has parked his truck nearby several times, always with a passenger or two inside. Waving his short arms toward their house, he wraps smiles around people Sal says are his customers.

"Bet he's trying to scare them," Sal mutters. "Warns that if they don't chuck everything old, they'll end up looking like us."

Just the other day Phee opened the front door, looked out in her pajamas, and had a thought. Wriggling her toes in the cool air, she wondered suddenly if her mom had done the same thing at age eleven. When *was* her mom coming home, anyway? It'd be good to have her around again, to talk about girl stuff and to help with the every-days, as they called the chores. While Phee stood there thinking, a neighbor walking by stared, his mouth open, then simply sped up. Not a word or a wave, even when she nodded hello.

"Stranger and stranger," as Sal put it. "No manners. The people coming out here now, some don't know where they are. They don't realize this is a community. A place where we notice each other."

It's not just the living that Sal notices. He can sometimes reason with unhappy ghosts in other people's homes, and he used to dowse for water using a willow stick, a skill that allowed people to dig a well in just the right spot. He can untie any problem and pick his way into most locks. He enjoys figuring out how to use almost anything left over. That includes modern materials like plastics or fiberglass, metals, and, of course, wood. All that floats or shelters . . . plus people.

Yes, people. He doesn't believe in all-bad souls, even the greediest ones. "Give 'em time," Sal likes to say.

Phee considers herself lucky to have a true islander for a grandfather, someone who has seen much sadness as well as joy. She knows that his parents, uncles, and aunts all died young, as did his wife, leaving him to live on as the only adult in a big house that was once filled. Phee has heard there were many mishaps in the family: a long-ago fall off a horse; a nasty tumble downstairs; boating accidents; something bad with a blacksmith's anvil; infections and diseases that had no cure. Before modern medicine, death was an everyday happening.

Sal is surprised by little.

When he steps back in the kitchen after visiting Mrs. Rebimbas that afternoon, he says nothing at first. He and the group of kids sit in a circle. The fire dances on their quiet, serious faces, dipping here a cheek, there a curl of hair, in gold and tarnished copper. Rose follows blue green as the flames leap and dart.

After a log falls in the fire and Sal pokes it back into place, the group hears a floorboard creak overhead. The Gang and the older man all look at the ceiling. Sal sighs.

"You'll be getting some help," he says slowly, "I do believe. But you kids will have to be careful. The tide that surrounds an old home can run high."

By the time all of the kids but Phee left the Folger house, the Gang had a plan. Sal gave it his blessing.

Like a doughnut with a hole in the middle, their idea was built around what was missing.

As we islanders know, empty space on Nantucket is rarely just that.

~

November 10.

Sal thought the Old North Gang had a plan to do just one thing: watch any ongoing damage, as Phee and Gabe had at Lydia Lyon's house. Stand in a close group at the edge of one property "renovation" after another, absorbing the details of wreckage. Remember and then tell, speaking to all the neighbors and residents who might listen.

They'd be out there after school and on weekends.

"You'll be peskier than a cloud of mosquitoes in August," Sal said to the group, looking pleased. "Mosquitoes with scarves and mittens."

When Phee and Gabe talked the next day, though, the plot began to deepen.

"Let's not disturb Sal with this," Phee said. "He's had enough worries in his life. But—"

One good thing about old friends is that ideas share themselves. "I know," Gabe said quickly. "Just standing around isn't enough.

"Last night, when I was falling asleep, I was startled awake by that boy in Mrs. Lyon's house, the one waving at me to hurry up. Like he could see me lying there in my warm bed. I felt awful when I realized he and the little girl and everyone else inside the front door will probably be gone for good in no time. The insides of that house are headed for the dump, right? Last night I pictured him standing in the dust of his home, his straw hat still on, broken bricks and splintered boards everywhere. He was *waiting* for me."

"Huh," Phee said, feeling just the tiniest bit spooked. "But not like, you know—"

"Not like I'm about to die or anything," Gabe finished for her.

"What did he want you to *do*?" Phee's voice was barely audible.

"I'm not sure," Gabe said. "I just know he wanted me to do more than stand and watch and then tattletale to people who already know this island has ghosts."

"What if it has something to do with your family stuff, like your great-grandma Hepsa's way of quieting spirits?"

Gabe looked nervous for the first time in their chat. "I think the boy wants me to be the lure," he said slowly. "Not to quiet things down, but to do the opposite."

"Yikes," Phee said. A shiver of fear slipped around her heart.

"Can't see turning away," Gabe said, sounding more like his dad than he knew. "I'll dive in."

❧

Mary here. When I was a girl, my grandmother made us doughnuts to be used as a spyglass. The modern spelling is *donut,* but I'll stick to the old.

If you were playing on the street—*whick-whacking around,* as some of us still say—you might smell something delicious coming from one of the houses. We kids always crept in closer, whispering, "So-and-so is making a plate of wonders."

The hope was that the door might open and the plate be passed around. No one ever cooks just one wonder.

Sometimes the grown-up in the kitchen teased us all by pretending not to know we were there. She might say by an open window, "I wonder what I'm going to do with all these today. Got too many. Maybe one of the dogs—"

That's when we'd pop out of the bushes, mouths watering, shouting, "NO, we're here!"

We kids would hold the warm, sugary circle up to one eye and look through the middle. When you spied a surprise, you sang out—like a seaman who spotted a whale—and were then allowed to eat that fried ring of bliss. People like Grandma Sue and Grandma Rebimbas must remember this, too. For us lookouts, it made us trim the wicks and keep our lanterns bright—that's kerosene-lamp talk.

Wonders prepared us for life.

We didn't miss much. Sometimes it was a fat slug that needed to be captured in the garden; other times a clot of dirt under a chair or a rip in the hem of a skirt. Things that were important to notice, clean up, or fix. Once I even found a British coin in the dirt and traded it for a chicken, to my grandmother's delight. No telling what a hungry soul can spot when looking through a wonder.

I'm glad that Gabe has been a part of the Old North Gang and eaten Grandma Sue's irresistible wonders.

Here's a bright bead of hope—hope that there is time for these kids to spot what they need to catch.

Hope that a boy can be a lure and also live to tell the story.

CHAPTER 10

A finger gathering snow

Sometimes kids need to take charge.

I say this with trepidation.

Our windless month is turning cold fast. On the evening of the eleventh, the island feels the first light dusting of snow.

Cyrus Coffin looks up from his math book, glancing out at the burial ground. He leans forward, squinting.

"Come here," he says quietly to Paul. Maddie is playing with plastic ponies on the bottom bunk across the room. She hops down and points outside. "They're walking," she says solemnly. "I seen it before, through the bushes."

Paul clicks off the overhead light in their bedroom, and the three kids press their noses to the window.

"This like what the twins saw that night?" Maddie asks.

"Dunno," Paul answers. "Doesn't seem like the same."

Maddie draws a lopsided smiley face on the condensation gathering on a windowpane.

Outside, a powdery snow is falling. Without a breath of wind, it should be drifting straight down, but instead it lands on several apparent but invisible objects in midair.

Look! Over there at the edge of the graveyard, is that the brief outline of a shoulder and the back of a head? Oh my, it's as round as a Halloween pumpkin. Only, there are no people to be seen, nor is there anything solid that might explain this.

"Are those *shadows*?" Cyrus whispers.

"Can't tell," Paul says quietly. "I don't think it's anything bad. But it feels—well, like they know we're here. *See?* That shape near the bushes just turned our way!"

"Yeah." Maddie nods. "And it likes us." She gives a little wave to the outlines, fingers opening and closing, and then goes back to playing on her bunk. Grabbing a pony with a baby-blue mane, she says, "I'm naming this one Benjamin. Benjamin Coffin."

The boys peer out in silence for a moment longer. Both see the grass rising and falling on its own, squishing down and then springing back up as if something unseen is stepping closer. Cyrus twitches the curtain closed.

"Better not be too obvious," he mutters to Paul, who nods but continues to peek through a crack.

The oldest of the boys sees an odd shape hovering at chest height in the curtain of snow, as if a man-sized hand were pointing at him, the side of it and one finger collecting flakes.

As if the ghost could see the boy's eye.

Paul Coffin steps back from the window, his heart hammering.

~

The temperature rises overnight and all snow is gone by dawn, leaving the ground wet.

As the Coffin kids wait by the side of the graveyard for the school bus the next morning, Paul nudges his brother.

"See that?" The three look down at what seem to be fresh footprints, many prints. Some are large and deep, as if made by a tall person. They weren't there yesterday.

"Maybe a school group." Cyrus bends to look. Both boys know that a visiting class would be made to walk through the main entrance to the cemetery.

"Someone with a stick," Paul says, pointing to a round hole pressed down into the mud.

"That's a wooden leg," Maddie announces promptly, as if identifying something as obvious as a pebble or a caterpillar.

Cyrus gives her a gentle shove. "How would *you* know?"

"I know," his little sister says, sticking out her tongue. As her brothers both look at her, she asks, "Hey, did Grandma make us cream cheese and jelly today? She'd better, because I'm giving Maria part of my sandwish. And hey, where ARE they this morning? The twins weren't sick *yesterday*. Sheesh. They're always late. Mariaaaaaaa!"

Maddie's voice warbles out over the quiet stones.

"Huh." Cyrus spins, peering in all directions, although he knows Maria and Markus will walk down only one particular footpath.

The quiet ones are good with a wonder, as I well know.

As the bus approaches, the Ramos twins hurry toward them, backpacks bouncing. Cyrus is busy staring at deep prints he's just noticed on a patch of bare ground not far from the oldest gravestones, the chipped ones covered with lichen. It's an area in which the five kids rarely play, as it's often boggy and damp.

Wait, he tells himself. *I'm not seeing this!*

I understand his concern. Steps made by bare feet after a snow? These are wide, man-sized toes, big ovals that point away from the graves and toward the road.

Not the twins. Not Cyrus or Paul or Maddie. Not a kid.

Who could have been out there without shoes on at this time of year? An unpleasant trickle of worry keeps him quiet.

The Ramos and Coffin kids pile onto the bus in a hurry, as the driver always seems impatient at their stop. There's a new kid from down the road, a girl who runs up at top speed at the last moment. She hasn't yet said hello and the driver practically slams the door after she's up the steps.

Today they slide past the girl and Maria smiles. The girl doesn't look friendly, but turns around to stare as the five kids sit down.

Choosing a seat of his own, Cyrus takes a moment to think. The footprints he's just seen belong with his grandma's words: *Nothing out there will ever hurt you. Just family.*

Really?

He wonders if relatives who died before you were born can recognize you.

He also wonders if, as family, they'd be nice. He thinks of the footsteps everyone heard yesterday at Phee's house.

Do relatives always know each other, or are they sometimes connected but apart, separated by time and space? Never actually touching?

Cyrus shakes his head, reminding himself that he's on the way to school and it's daytime. He can hear what Grandma Sue might say: "For heaven's sake, stop worrying about a bunch of footprints!"

Slouching in his seat, he tries.

CHAPTER 11

All you ghosts

Courage can go wrong. I want to sit down on a rock and think, but my job isn't to do that. It's to spread the news while I'm here.

I am the town's Crier today, but as you know, I will be silent—dead silent—if my home is destroyed.

Gone and dead are two different things, with the first stronger than the last.

I'm not trying to scare you away—I want you to *stay.*

Hunting for what may help to save the soul of this island means sorting, and it's like cleaning out a sewing basket. What will be needed? Which past buttons to keep? Which present tangles to toss? I wish I knew all the answers. I certainly don't.

But I do know one truth: We islanders tend to stay.

In the old days, plenty lived and died on this tiny island and never set foot on the mainland. Of course, the whaling crews and their officers sailed far, far away, but most came hurrying back, sat in the kitchen, and smoked pipe after pipe. Islanders are proud of their distinct speech, habits, and homes, and most seem content to be just where they are in the world, on this scrubby patch of sand.

They might complain about bad weather or a fence the neighbor put up, but unless forced, few leave.

They don't have the same need for change that many on the mainland have, and until recently this included a calm sense of *this is ours*. For many decades we natives were able to gather money from visitors and send them packing, no harm done. It was a harvest, like catching fish, raking for quahog clams, or gathering greens.

Let's face it. Nantucketers cling to this sandy soil with an intensity that borders on obsession. The Quaker houses in the old part of town are tightly clustered but refuse to line up. The streets wiggle and wander, and gardens and yards—rarely rectangular—bump and drift around the gray shingles. Front doors are set so that each of us looks out at our own angle. It's as if we care about each other but remain thorny. Or is it solitary?

Sal and Phee live this way.

Come to think of it, that's just how the scalloping fleet works. The small boats are outfitted with heavy nets and a culling board, most of the rigs made by hand. The fleet looks out for one another's safety, but each boat works on its own. The scallopers respect territory.

As on water, so on land: There's a harrumph to these houses. A knock-first message. Perhaps that is the key to all kinds of survival around here, including mine.

Does it explain our population of ghosts?

Any resident will tell you that we like to do things our own way.

The Old North Gang knows this.

I do, too.

Ours has always been an island of immigrants, starting with the English settlers in the 1600s, many of whom are relatives of Sal's and Phee's. And mine, come to think of it. There were also the Cape Verdeans, who came in the eighteenth century from a cluster of Portuguese islands. They still have many descendants, most with other backgrounds stirred in, like the Rebimbas and Ramos families.

And now little Nantucket is bursting at the seams with energetic newcomers, folks who work hard and save lots of what they earn but can't find a place to settle down.

Many arrive, camp out for months or even years in cars, garages, or with friends, and then give up and leave, exhausted by the housing struggle. These workers make me think of hermit crabs, those brave creatures that move from empty shell to empty shell—snail to moon to conch—as they grow, sometimes having to compete with one another for shelter. There's desperation to this drama. Some end up with nothing and are eaten by other crabs or a passing bird.

I've heard that many of the island's working population have no place to live. No one knows the exact number, but during summer it's said to be easily hundreds of souls.

It's a dark secret in the middle of the wonder.

The same thing happens to one wave of hopeful workers after another. People travel from around the world to find jobs, providing services that tourists and residents want, then fall in love with the place just as our ancestors did, and want to stay for good. They come from countries on other islands, like the Dominican Republic, Jamaica, or Haiti; from Central and South America, Northern and Eastern Europe, and even Russia. I'm told a few are from Asia. At last count, the public school has families speaking eleven distinct languages.

The school wants to make room for all. But a family can't live at school.

In the old days, many found an unused boat and cast anchor in one of the harbors or hitched up to the wharves. No one minded—that is, if you didn't party too much and could ride out the storms. It was normal to see underwear and work shirts drying on the rails or rigging on a sunny morning.

That worked well for Phee's mom and dad, until it didn't.

Now the rules in the harbor are stricter. Homemade houseboats are discouraged. The fancy boats have multiplied, crowding out many others.

Phee is growing up with a big home and a deep tangle of island roots. When she started at the elementary school, other kids with Caribbean parents asked her how long she'd been on Nantucket.

She always said she'd been born at sea, in a boat, but that wasn't the whole story and she knew it.

In first grade, she asked her grandfather some questions. "Sal, how long has our family lived here?"

"Depends how you look at it. On your mom's side, over three hundred years, and on your dad's side, not long. Why?"

"Kids ask."

"Oh." Sal looked thoughtfully at his granddaughter. "What do you say?"

"That I was born on a boat. Then they don't ask anymore."

Sal scratched his head and his eyes twinkled. "Easier that way."

Phee nodded.

"But not the full truth," her grandfather added, placing an arm around his granddaughter.

Phee ducked her head. "I feel sad for my friends who talk about no home. They really want one, more than anything. Some of them spend the summer in a truck with no tires or an empty school bus. A girl in my class cried because she doesn't want to move again. Her family's cottage got taken away and now they live in a shed that smells bad. Her mattress goes under the table at night. I saw her mom blinking fast and making smears on her cheeks when she talked to our teacher outside the classroom."

Mary Chase here! I blink and fight tears also, remembering both the pain of losing my family's home and the relief, later on, of having my own place for so many decades. Sometimes I think home is everything.

Sal sat back and looked as though an idea was rising in his mind like the summer sun, dazzling as it became brighter.

"Let's *do* something about it," he said to his granddaughter. "Together. Shake on it!" He offered Phee a calloused, weathered hand, and she grinned, holding out her fist for a bump.

"Like *this*, silly Sal," she said, and showed him.

That was six years ago.

Soon families and single adults without housing began staying with Sal and Phee for stretches of time. All were welcome, as long as they could live as the Folgers did.

Many couldn't.

Sal cooks on a woodstove and uses oil lamps for light at night. When his taxes went up many years ago and he had difficulty paying the gas and electric bills, he dusted off the old glass lamps lined up on a shelf in the basement and began chopping wood. He turned off the heat and cleaned his grandparents' cooking stove, which had only been used recently in a here's-how-we-used-to-do-it way, for drying sliced apples and cranberries during the holidays.

In winter, Sal and Phee use both the old wood-fired kitchen stove and several working fireplaces, and their windows dance with a warm, rosy light missing from most other houses.

Sal welcomes into their home any local who needs

housing, and many land in one of the upstairs bedrooms for a time. People staying with them help out with the everydays, but without an Internet connection, most of their guests have difficulty; also, sleeping at the Folger home means doing some heavy lifting, working in the garden if it's that time of year, getting used to old plumbing and cooking methods, using hot water sparingly, carting clothes and bedding to the Laundromat or washing them in a tub and then hanging them out to dry—and on top of that, putting in long hours at a paying job. Although Sal never wants money for his hospitality, most guests don't stay long. Come to think of it, no strangers have knocked on their door in over a year.

This is strange, as the housing crunch on Nantucket has reached an emergency level. Lots of businesses offer a place for summer workers to live, but there aren't nearly enough rentals to go around in the winter. Many residents have been trying to help, but solutions are hard to come by. Affordable land is limited, and owning a home here is, for most, a distant dream.

As islanders say, the housing shuffle gets old fast. You'd think a free place to stay would always be packed.

Phee and Sal are puzzled that the number of people staying with them has dropped off, and think it might be the ghosts in their house.

In some cultures, ghosts are terrifying. People from the Caribbean and Eastern Europe, in particular, don't like the idea of cohabiting with ghosts. Several families left the Folger home abruptly, bundling their clothing higgledy-piggledy onto bikes and into cars. Not wanting to offend Sal, they didn't exactly explain why. A look of shock, a vibe of fear—their faces told the story.

Sal grew up with layers of ghosts. The Folger house was first owned by sea captains and whaling merchants. Then, after Nantucket's depression, it passed to a cooper, a banker, and housewrights—a *wright* meaning a master carpenter like Sal. Births and deaths inside those walls were a part of life. For all families at the time, pain and happiness chased each other, and most of that drama happened at home.

Until well into the twentieth century, people didn't go to the Nantucket Cottage Hospital to have a baby or die, and children witnessed much more than they do today. Screams, tears, bravery, and loss were all a part of it.

The Folgers collected oil paintings, silver and china, furniture, scrimshaw, sailors' valentines made with shells from around the world, embroidery, and many other things. As the house was never sold, each generation kept what it wanted, which was just about everything that hadn't turned to dust.

Sal was raised understanding that home was a place still filled with the family who came before. His grandmother used to rock and knit by the kitchen stove on winter evenings; even when she was old and bedridden, she refused to allow her chair to be moved. She insisted that her basket of wool and her bundle of whalebone needles stay right on the seat and that it point southeast, toward all who'd gone to sea and never come home.

After she died, the chair rocked on its own if anyone moved the basket. Sal remembers his mother speaking gently to it and gesturing to the seat. Finally the chair quieted.

It's still there, and Sal and Phee both like to use it. The worn rockers are as smooth as can be, and the chair practically moves itself. Phee suspects that she gets a helpful push sometimes while rocking, because she's the latest child.

She loves hearing Sal's ghost stories, which are both shivery and cozy. He remembers his grandmother speaking to a wall of paintings owned by her recently deceased husband, a collection of paintings of hands. She needed to take down and then rehang the collection in order to replace stained wallpaper, but wanted to reassure those who'd collected the hands—her husband and his father—that the art wasn't going anywhere.

"See?" Sal heard her saying. "We're just moving these to fix the room. Nothing is leaving." As soon as she spoke, one of the paintings lifted itself off a hook and dropped gently onto a chair.

As a boy, Sal was curious about the hands. His grandmother explained that Nantucket had been built by hand and we'd be nowhere without the creativity of so many workers, hands that fished and planted and carved and built. The Folgers, she said, never forget that.

Sal still lives with most of the paintings of hands. He has his favorites. Some hold a tool, a weapon, or jewelry; others pray or point; still others reach for another hand. To make ends meet, he's had to sell a few of the more valuable European ones, along with some of the silver that he and Phee never use. However, he holds on to everything he can.

After his mother died, Sal heard the sounds of her calling his name, sometimes tearfully. Mostly at night, while his father snored, Sal caught her voice drifting through the rooms. His father, never an easy man, was ill by then and slept so heavily that nothing woke him.

Sal told Phee this story: "I walked through the house with a lamp, talking to her. I let her know that I wouldn't leave again, and that when I married, my children and grandchildren would be here. I also told her that I'd care for my father for the rest of his life, which I did."

Here Sal paused, looking troubled. "I'll never know if that was the right thing to do, but family is family."

"What do you mean, Sal?"

"Well, it's like the roots of our oldest trees in town, the ones that slowly heave the brick sidewalks or interrupt fences. We don't get rid of them when they don't behave. Sometimes we love them even more."

"Huh," Phee said. "And my grandma Polly, your wife and Mom's mother, died here in the kitchen, right?"

"Right," Sal said. "Complications after childbirth. I was out working, and my father—Well, who knows." He was quiet for a beat, studying the low rafters in the room where he and Phee spent most of their time.

"This house is us," he said quietly. "Sadness and all."

"And—" Phee paused, curious but not wanting to upset her grandfather. "Is Polly still here?"

Sal squinted at Phee, as if measuring how much to tell her. "Hmm," he said slowly, "she may be. Shortly after Polly died, my father passed, too. Then it was just me and your mom—little Flossie—in this big house. I needed help with the baby, and I have to think my Polly was still here with me. The fire in the kitchen stove was always burning brightly before I came down in the morning, and sometimes when Flossie woke in the night, in the room next to mine, I'd hear Polly singing softly to her."

"*Really* singing?" Phee asked.

Sal nodded. "And it worked. Flossie went right back to sleep."

"So that's not sad," Phee said. "I mean, the ghost stuff is sometimes happy."

Sal straightened his sock hat. "*Happy* is too easy a word, but I think that sadness in a house can change into something else if you allow it to, like rubbing oil into wood to make it shine. It isn't just oil anymore. It becomes part of the beauty of the wood. Beautiful things don't always smile."

"So, Sal, the ghost visits come and go, right?"

"Right." Sal rubbed his hands together as they talked. "And sometimes a ghost will appear to one member of the family but not another. Flossie used to say when she was around your age that she knew an older man was watching over her during the day if she was in our house alone while I was out doing an errand. She described a man with a white beard and big hairy ears, someone who peeked around corners in a raggedy sweater and smiled. He sounded to me just like my father. And when Flossie saw this man, she felt safe. He was reassuring. Kindly."

"And you never saw him?"

"Nope. He wasn't a friendly man in life—at least not to me," Sal said slowly.

"So sometimes ghosts can care for one person in the family but not another?" Phee asked. "Or make things better, even if they didn't when they were alive?"

"Exactly." Sal nodded. "And sometimes they're around for a while, when needed, and then they're gone for decades but later return. I'll never pretend to understand how it all works, but I do think they try to help us out."

"Hey, *ghosts*!" Phee called suddenly. "All you ghosts! Please help us to find homes for more families, can you?"

I recognized Phee's strong feelings about home. She is a child who understands the sting of loss.

The kitchen was silent for a moment . . . and then a handbell sitting on the windowsill rang, a clear *diiiiing!*

As Phee gave Sal a wide-eyed look, feet clumped down the stairs outside the kitchen door, *boom-boom-bam*, as if wearing loose fishing boots.

Sal hopped up and peered out the back door. He shook his head.

"Just like Flossie," murmured Sal. "Funny, she used to walk heavily on those steps and loved borrowing my boots. One of these days she'll be back with us. Sometimes I think the house sends out remembered sounds for no reason at all, to fill the corners. Maybe it was *you* who did it, calling to the ghosts just now. Well . . . Your mother will be pleased about what we're trying to do, I know that."

"Think she's okay?" Phee asked, her voice small.

"Of course I do." Her grandfather's voice was deep and calm. "As I said, this home of ours sometimes chimes in."

Both sat in silence for a moment, watching the embers glow in the kitchen stove.

"My dad was an immigrant here," Phee noted, as if finishing a thought. "Maybe that's why Jules and Flossie didn't live with you, even when you asked. Maybe that's why he went back to Haiti. The ghosts in the house."

Another silence. "I think it was something between the two of them, plus your mother's need to be independent," Sal said. He looked tired. "We Folgers rarely forget that we were immigrants at one time, too," he added.

Neither noticed that all three of the inside doors to the kitchen had drifted wide open, as if the house was listening.

CHAPTER 12

A brick flies, a boy is gone

November 12.

As far as Sal knows, the kids in the Old North Gang are beginning their work today, standing on the sidelines and reporting.

They return to Lydia Lyon's house. My heart beats faster.

"GO!" I shout to them. "Closer!"

In the last three days, a dumpster has been filled to the top with old boards and beams. Eddy Nold now plans to lift the entire house, resting it on scaffolding in order to dig out the basement, a job that buys us some time, as they are ignoring what's left of the upper floors.

The very sight of all that ugly destruction makes me fluttery with fear. Hollower than the hollowest pumpkin.

Men circle the foundation, pointing and talking. A

bulldozer sits idle nearby. Now the contractor marches around the corner.

"There." He points. "Start by that huge fieldstone. I'll just step inside to see whether—" His voice is muffled as he ducks in what was once the front door and looks up at the chimney. A brick shoots down from above, hitting him on the forehead.

"Holy creepers!" he shouts, and backs away. One boot plunges beneath the flooring. Suddenly he's down on his knees, sunglasses hanging from one ear, blood trickling from a cut above his eyebrow, eyes almost as big as Mrs. Rebimbas's wonders.

"You okay in there, boss?" one of the workers asks.

"Sure thing," Eddy says, staggering out. He dabs at his forehead and brushes off his pants. A loud giggle comes from nowhere, and the Nold group spins around. The Gang look just as surprised. The adults frown. The kids nod hello to the adults, but there's no response.

One of the workers covers his mouth and then clears his throat, turning away.

Eddy narrows his eyes. "Let's just get this dig launched," he barks.

"Why aren't they making us leave?" Markus whispers to Paul.

"Because we're small," Maddie whispers with a grin.

"Speak for yourself." Cyrus pokes her.

"She is," Maria snaps back.

Tempers are wearing thin.

~

An hour later, the site is deserted minus the kids and Eddy Nold's truck.

Once Eddy gave the order to begin excavation, the bulldozer's ignition stuck and then the on-site generator blew. It looked to me like sabotage—but whether or not there were ghosts behind it, I couldn't say.

I don't seem able to see spirits the way Gabe does.

Shaking his head, Eddy sent his workers home early and retreated to sit in his truck, dab at his head, and make phone calls.

"That's what I'm saying," he shouted, his voice carrying through glass. "Crazy, just everything going wrong. Yep, yep, that's right, we're taking a slow-down day. Tomorrow, sure thing."

The Gang had wandered quietly to the back of the house as Eddy talked, hoping he wouldn't notice. Gabe stood next to Phee, looking up at the second floor.

Suddenly he stiffened, squinted, and raised a hand as if to say, *Be right there*. Phee touched his shoulder. "Careful," she said softly.

Gabe nodded and opened the back door. The interior

looked dark and gloomy. He stepped inside, and the house seemed to swallow him whole.

~

While Gabe is in Lydia Lyon's house, Eddy drives off. I flip back through time, running my fingers over the days. I do this when I'm nervous and unable to ring or call out.

Hands can speak.

It was Phee who came up with the name Nantucket Hands over a year ago.

"That's it, Sal! Let's start a kind of adventure club, only it'll be for people of all ages who are struggling to stay here, you know?"

The idea began back when she and her grandfather first bumped fists, when she was a little girl.

"Mmm . . ." Sal was examining a leaky window. "Like the name. And how will this club help folks out?"

"By making people care about each other. And believe everything will fall into place," Phee said promptly. "Like you always do for me."

"I do?" Sal grinned at her. "Now, what makes you think *that*?"

Phee poked her grandfather. "Come on, you silly! You even make ghosts sound normal."

"Which they are," Sal added.

Over the next hour, they sat on the steps of the Folger house and made a plan.

By spring, Nantucket Hands would begin its work: uniting people who were struggling to earn a living in the island trades, wanted to stay, but didn't qualify for affordable housing. Helping them share with, and gather strength from, one another and *then*—and this mattered a great deal to Sal and Phee—find the right footing to work toward having year-round homes.

Sal hoped for funds so that the group could go on expeditions. These might include a picnic at Altar Rock—the highest hill in the moors—a trip to the Lifesaving Museum, or perhaps even a day of fishing. A visit to the so-called Oldest House, built in 1686, or a clambake on a remote beach. Everyone would return to their everyday lives feeling less alone. That, and proud of the special island they called home, whether or not they had been born here.

Sal wished that everyone in Nantucket Hands would grow to recognize herself or himself in the history of the place. Without being mushy, he would send out the message that friends mattered and that to live by your hands on this island was to belong.

"I don't have all the answers, Phee," he had warned her at the start. "This island is a dot in the ocean, and there won't be room for every single person who wants to stay and work, you know? There's no overflow town down the road, like on the mainland. But we who live here can do better at honoring *the ways we lived in the past,* not just telling stories about them. We could begin by *not destroying* any more of the strongholds of our ghosts, places as unchanged as this house, and not forgetting that they were built by people who knew how to survive. Boy, did they know how! The past might hold more solutions than people realize."

"Do ghosts get things done?" Phee asked, her hands on her hips.

"Well now, if you don't scare them away, they might," Sal said.

I must say, I agree! Ghosts, like the Gang, will not give up easily.

Has Nantucket Hands gone on an actual adventure? I am the Crier, but admit that I can't keep track of everything at every moment, nor can I do much about how busy things get around here, even in a windless November.

At any rate, joining hands is forever a good thing, as Mrs. Rebimbas knew, and it could help us through these dangerous times.

Nantucket has a bouquet of cultures it couldn't claim in my day. Perhaps that jumble of languages and hopes will save us all.

Unlike many kids growing up here now, I, Mary W. Chase, only ever spoke plain old English, although we learned some Latin in the schools. "Latin will make you learned," my aunt used to say as she snapped beans or pared potatoes. Knowing I couldn't seem to spell or read easily, she'd say *learn-ed* as if it were two words, leaning on the syllables. I was clumsy with a knife and slow at school, mostly because my head was filled with other things.

Aunt Thankful had spent her adult life caring for elderly parents, and was always trying to improve me. In an effort to make me a better person, she forced me to sit quietly in the house, hands in my lap, for at least an hour a day.

Was she trying to make me like her? I don't think it worked.

Her slowing me down inside only made me more determined to escape. I was happiest on my own and thoughtful around all the things that made me curious, like the language of clouds or how a crow can become friends with a human.

Meeting kids from far-off parts of the world might have made me less shy. I could've spent time with others who were also asking questions.

I might've had a voice while I was alive.

CHAPTER 13

The ways of crows

Gabe waved hello to someone unseen before stepping into the Lyon home. Who was it?

I can't help wishing that Gabe were a powerful crow with wings and not a boy! I'd feel better if he wasn't alone with ghosts in a wreck of a house.

He and the others have a brave plan, that's for sure. While Gabe is inside, the Gang waits wordlessly outside Mrs. Lyon's place, looking at a building and yard that were once filled with laughter and the patter of small feet. What happened to all the good smells of stew cooking in a big pot, the dance of clothes drying on the line, the chatter of a garden in bloom?

Where does the busy beat of living go when it's gone?

The kids whisper together as the afternoon darkens, wondering if it's time to chase their friend.

Why am I thinking of crows, those birds that fear few others and become invisible at night?

I realize crows have lots in common with lonely kids. Not *lonely*—that sounds bad. Grown-alone kids. Like me and like Phee. Or Flossie. Or Sal. Or Gabe. All raised as the only kid in a home.

Crows are survivors. Like Criers, they announce what matters.

If a person is mean to a crow, that crow will be mean back. I'm telling the truth. They will shriek and sometimes even dive on nasty people. I once saw a crow grab the feather off a neighbor's hat, but only after she'd waved her arms and scared the birds away from her crab apple tree. And for no reason, as she wasn't using the apples that year; her yard was a carpet of delicious reds.

That woman never did it again.

The house my aunt Thankful lived in all her life has a millstone in the backyard. A big, flat rock once brought to the island by a miller who lived there before her parents did. He had ordered the wrong size for one of the four island windmills, and so he carted it home. To me it was a table. It's still there.

I picked daisies and braided them right on that flat, smooth top. I took my dolls for walks around the edges and lined up treasures I'd pocketed while running around, objects like a nail twisted into a question mark, a chipped bit of crystal from a lamp, or a bright shard of crockery, finds that jumped out underfoot. In those days, people threw broken household goods out back, so there was plenty to discover.

Crows always notice what is in a person's hand, and they do like a sparkle.

One day I was sitting on the millstone having a snack while my aunt hung the bedsheets. A crow watched me eat. First his head went one way and then the other. His eyes were bright and shining, like bits of polished coal.

Very quietly—Aunt Thankful would have been angry if she'd seen me wasting good food—I put a bite-sized piece of bread next to a blue-and-gold chip of china, something I had found. I looked at the crow and tapped the spot with my finger. Then I stood up and walked away.

The crow watched me and also my aunt, who hadn't noticed what I'd done.

Minutes later we were inside, folding shirts. I was peeking out the window.

The crow swooped down and ate the bread. Then he

looked at the chip, turning his head from side to side. He picked it up in his beak and flew away.

The next day, there was a bright-red bead on the millstone, right on that spot. Truly, it made me as happy as if he'd left a ruby.

The crow and I were great friends from that moment on. We gave each other many presents—opalescent buttons, a twist of shiny ribbon, the handle from a daffodil-yellow teacup, a silver buckle missing its tongue, a bent hat pin. I always kept the crow's gifts carefully arranged in ocean clamshells sitting on the millstone. I called it my museum. It stayed outside except in bad weather, and the crow never took back what he'd already given.

My aunt couldn't admit he was special, but she left my museum alone. One day, the crow didn't return and I had no idea why.

Aunt Thankful didn't talk about sadness, instead treating it like a rotten spot in a turnip. Something to carve out and toss away. I looked for my crow for years, and somehow the story of my crow and me became known around town when I was growing up.

Sal heard the story from his parents, and decades later, he told Phee. She began watching crows in the backyard trees.

Have you heard the term *a murder of crows*, meaning a group of crows? It goes back to the 1400s in Europe, and might date to the fact that crows sometimes snack on dead creatures. Or perhaps it's just their rough cry, size, and deep-black feathers.

Maybe it's all of the above, plus the fact that crows reason and remember, making them capable of murder.

After my crow vanished, I felt better when I thought about him being so tough.

~

Still no Gabe. But oddly, a crow now flies overhead, circles the Lyon house, and alights on a nearby tree. I see Phee squinting at the bird.

I peer, too, feeling guilty. I hope with all my heart that Gabe can work with the ghosts inside, and that they save the Lyon house *and then mine.*

Selfish of me, I know.

Maybe I'm not that important. Perhaps a crow could be just as good at being a Crier.

"Hey!" I call to the crow. "Can you help that boy? Will you help us all? I'm the girl who made friends with someone in your family long ago!" The bird looks down at me, black eyes gleaming. He turns his head to one side and then the other, as if to be sure it's really me.

He flaps his wings, looking larger than life. I step back. Now a closer sound, a stumble-thump: A boy pops out through the door. Gabe! In one piece! The other members of the Gang surround him in a rush. I try to eavesdrop but can't hear what he's saying.

I look up, wanting to thank the crow. It's gone.

I slump, relieved but worn by worry, and settle for seeing the Gang hurry off together, Gabe in the middle. I look back toward the silent Lyon house but see no other children.

Now Gabe raises a hand in a see-you-later way. My heart jumps for just a moment, until I remember the other ghosts nearby. No, I'm not seen.

The crow soars between us and cuts off my view. It circles by as if to say, *That's enough for now. No more curiosity. Take your bead and go!*

I do, spreading the news.

~

People here talk about "the Nantucket way," which means giving what's needed, but not in a showy manner.

More like a crow or like Sal.

He always made enough for his family to get by on through word of mouth, although how that worked was something of a mystery. He'd fix a roof or seal a leak in the bottom of a boat and then refuse to leave a bill. Friends knew what to do. Either they'd leave an envelope with cash in the Folger mail basket by the front door or start delivering a bunch of fish or vegetables. Sal rarely said thank you. Nor did he expect anyone to say it to him.

He'd be out on a job and someone might stop by and ask casually if he could fix their rotten porch. While he was working on that porch, a neighbor down the street might leave a note on his bike, asking him to please replace a few storm windows when he had the time. One thing led to another.

"Once an islander, always an islander," Sal explained to Phee when she asked him why he liked patching instead of doing work that paid regular money. "Kids born here have a lifelong advantage. They understand, from day one, that a life can be built this way." Sal paused, looking down at his scarred palms.

Phee knows every line on those hands. She can close her eyes and picture them without seeing.

"It's our way of being human," Sal added. "And it's efficient. These old houses were built to survive, and their materials actually last longer and adapt better than most modern materials. An old wooden house expands and shrinks; it understands how to be moist and then dry without damage; it *breathes*. Very little is absolutely flat or level, which does confuse some people. Take the lime-based plaster made with ground oyster shells and horsehair, the stuff that's still on our walls here; it absorbs both noise and moisture better than drywall. And these old wooden beams and floors that came from first-growth American trees: This is denser and therefore stronger lumber, and because it changes with the seasons, it lasts. Some young folks in construction don't know that, and honestly think *old* equals *weak*.

"No sirree. Not around here." Sal grinned.

I grinned, too.

CHAPTER 14

Things get crazier

Recently, Sal has noticed something very odd happening toward the back of the Folger property.

Boards and pieces of trim from other old houses seem to be appearing on their own. The pile grows daily. All are used and a few are the valuable, really wide kind, obviously cut a long time ago from giant trees. None are rotten. It's as if someone picked through the old lumber being discarded and passed along the very best pieces.

Sal has had people offer him useful odds and ends, but never sneak them unseen into the Folger yard.

Meanwhile, workers have begun to report dumpsters filled with old wood being emptied overnight, plus a few unexplained bumps and bangs at the "renovation" sites that are the source. Angry footsteps and loud thumps have been heard with no one nearby, ladders have wobbled, tools been dropped, lifted, or thrown. Carpenters, painters, electricians, and plumbers have sworn they were pushed or tripped, and complain of minor injuries. Sal, as one known to settle ghosts, is surprised no contractor has stopped him on the street to ask what he thinks.

He wonders if the more aggressive builders, those like Eddy Nold, have been told there is no such thing as ghosts. Truth is, Sal isn't sure how anyone can stop Eddy. He didn't want to say that either to the Gang or to Mrs. Rebimbas, but he can admit it to himself.

Outrage is powerful, as are the island's spirits, but mixing the two won't guarantee change.

Troubled, Sal paces at home while the Gang visits Lydia Lyon's house. *Bam, bam!* Someone knocks on the kitchen door. Sal throws it open.

It's Gabe's dad, Herbie Pinkham. He and Flossie were friends when the two were children, and Sal is pleased to see him.

"Here in official capacity, Sal," Herbie says.

"Ah." Sal rocks back on his heels, suddenly fearful for the kids. He doubts Herbie knew they were headed out to observe dangerous work sites, and on their own.

Herbie, sensing Sal's discomfort, says quickly, "It's about the boards out back."

"Oh, *well*! Come on in." Sal throws open the door. "Something bigger than us is at work, Herbie." Sal is now striding toward the back-porch door. "Glad to show you."

"Happy to hear it." The officer is right behind him. "Whoa!" Herbie backs up at the sight of all that lumber. "Got some wood here! That's a lotta hauling. And it's making a mess of trouble for me."

"Me, too." Sal nods. "Don't know what to do with it. So I guess word is out."

"And you didn't take it?" Herbie looks puzzled. "People are saying it means you're on the sites with all the accidents."

"And that I'm the problem?" Sal snorts and throws his arms wide, bumping a chair nearby, which then rocks angrily on its own. Herbie's eyes move with it, slowly widening.

"The next thing you know, they'll be confusing the living with the dead!" Sal says, his eyes twinkling.

"Hmph," Herbie mumbles. Surprising himself, he wishes suddenly that he and his grandmother could have a heart-to-heart chat about ghosts. One his wife and son knew nothing about.

As if reading his mind, Sal says, "Your granny Pinkham."

Herbie's head snaps up and he studies Sal's face. "Just thinking of her," he says gruffly.

Sal is now pacing again. "She'd say, 'There's someone wants to be noticed. So give 'em what they want.'"

Herbie looks around the old kitchen but says nothing. He sighs.

"Herbie," Sal says gently, "be who you are."

~

"You okay? What happened? Who did you see?" The voices chime and tumble around him.

At first Gabe is speechless, but he's soon filling in the Gang, who huddle close, mouths open like so many fish.

Here is what he tells them:

When he stepped inside the Lyon house, leaving his buddies in a nervous group outside, he called softly, "Helloooo? You guys still here? So what can we do? I'm back! Here to help."

Taking a couple of steps into the front parlor, he placed a hand on what was left of the fireplace mantel.

For a moment the house was quiet and then he heard a sudden *shrump-scuffle*, as if someone were squeezing through a tight space. The boy and girl again appeared on the second floor, peeking down through splintered walls.

Gabe had been prepared to be frightened but instead felt that same flush of excitement he'd had on the beach. A connection—*I am here, and so are they!*

The girl was Maddie's age, and held up her doll to show Gabe. She danced it up and down, making its china slippers clack. Still wearing his hat, the boy took a step closer, pulling the girl, then turned away and looked around at the house.

Next, he spun back toward Gabe as if impatient for him to understand.

"What?" Gabe asked. The stairs to the second floor were gone. "I can't fly up there."

Wheee! Gabe had the odd sensation of being blown sideways toward a wall, but gently. Soon his shoulder was against what remained of a bare corner post, and he saw what was left of the keeping room, the main living space in a very old house, filling up with life.

Like foam at the tide line, one scene after another shimmered and then popped around him. He watched a grandma mending a sock by the fire, an old dog at her feet. A toddler sat nearby, playing with spoons and a kettle. *Pop!* Suddenly they were replaced by another scene, one with holly on the mantel, stockings hanging by a fire, and a row of kids standing nearby, their eyes dizzy with Christmas. *Pop!* Now Gabe saw a young woman washing the floor with a rag and singing, at the same time, to a baby in a cradle. *Pop!* He saw the boy and his sister. They were younger, watching as a woman who looked like their mother rolled out pie dough on the kitchen table. Nearby was a bowl filled with sugared cranberries. Smiling, she pulled off a chunk of dough for each of them, and they busily flattened and shaped it with small fingers, then reached toward the berries. *Pop!* Gabe realized he was alone again, the house silent and cold.

He looked back at where the boy and girl had first appeared, on the second floor. Although they seemed to be gone, he whispered, "Thanks. I know you're with me, and—"

Just then, Gabe felt a push and stumbled out the front door. He knew in a flash that he'd said the wrong thing.

After all, he hadn't yet given what these ghost kids wanted from him. Was he right to think they liked the Gang's plan?

Outside in the cold, surrounded by his friends, Gabe sorts through an odd mix of discomfort at having assumed too much, relief at being back in the everyday world, and excitement about getting to the next house.

At the moment, I can tell he is no longer afraid, but I am.

Like a kid who swims on a calm day and imagines the waters are always kind, he's not wary.

I think of my house, standing intact near Lydia Lyon's, innocent of what may come. Hope of a rescue is colored by fear.

I shiver, both for my home and for this boy.

Maybe some of this is my fault for waking and then ringing and hollering. For spreading the news.

The Gang's plan is to visit as many houses that are "under attack" as they can, dangling Gabe as the lure.

No adults, including Sal, are to know.

But, of course, I know. Do I count, even if no one knows I'm here?

CHAPTER 15

Stones and pinches

November 15, and still no wind.

While the Gang plan their next visit, the rest of the island shifts uneasily. No one living remembers a full two weeks with not even the whisper of a breeze. People's thoughts are loud in their heads.

Many aren't sleeping well. They startle awake, thinking they've heard an odd footstep or a rustling outside their windows. During the day, they drop dishes, spill food, make mistakes at work.

Islanders find odd questions coming to mind, such as: *How do you best use a splintered lifesaving oar that's washed up on the beach? Is there a favorite island recipe for cooking and eating boat shell snails, also known as slipper shells?* Those are the little shells that look like a tiny rowboat, or perhaps a shoe. Or *Should I be out lane-ing*—an old phrase that means wandering in the narrow streets in town—*during the next full moon?*

If they're adults, they laugh and push these thoughts away.

Not the kids. They are listening.

Lately, a flood tide of old Nantucket names floats incessantly through their heads, names of people they don't know.

Math goes undone. Chores are neglected at home. The kids seem to be carried along on an unseen current. A source of some kind is at work, one that is filling young minds and hearts with an insistence that can't be ignored.

Irritated parents and teachers realize, after several tries, that the kids are not ignoring them. Rather, they are busy, paying attention to details that matter, even if they don't yet know why or how.

Today, Gabe thinks about Peleg Hussey, Hepsabeth Gardner, and Josiah Turner. Maria and Markus are stuck at the moment on Hezekiah and Tristram Starbuck, and as Maria had thought of one name, and Markus the other, they wonder if the Starbucks are also twins.

At school, the kids scribble a name or two on the covers of their notebooks, on the edges of workbook pages, even on the palms of their hands. The names change hourly, with the new displacing the old as if that were natural, like shells shifting at the tide line.

Oh my! I've just heard Markus muttering the name of my late husband, Daniel B. Chase. He was not a great companion, but I do believe I'm starting to forgive him. The more I ring my bell and blow my horn, the more I realize he must have done the best he could. He was wounded in the Civil War, lost a leg, and died decades later, at age seventy-nine, in our house, peacefully, on a day when the wind banged and whistled so hard that he thought it was distant cannons.

My Daniel must be pleased he's here in the story. That, and surprised to see *me* as the Crier.

One curious teacher decides to stop at the Historical Association library after school with a long list of these names. She soon discovers that they all belong to Nantucketers from the past, mostly everyday people who didn't make it into the history books. All are buried here.

Leaning back in her chair, she lets the import of this news sink in. *There's a missing link,* she thinks to herself. *If these were plain old people, how did the kids get their names?*

She looks around the Historical Association library

and then glances at the librarian, on his computer in the corner. *Better not to ask*, she warns herself. *Not yet.*

Walking out the door, she runs across Sal, a font of information for all things Nantucket. She begins to understand . . . or so she thinks.

Cyrus Coffin finds himself thinking about Shubael Brock and Benjamin Whippey, his brother Paul about Lucy Coffin and Enoch Gardner. When the boys ask their sister, Maddie, if she has any names in her head, she answers promptly, "Lydia Barker. Woof!"

Phoebe Antoine has been hearing *Walter Folger, Walter Folger* over and over. She knows this is a famous name in her family.

"Who is Walter Folger?" she asks Sal. "I forgot."

"There've been a few, but the most famous one was an island cousin who lived on Pleasant Street a long time ago, a self-taught inventor and mathematician," her grandfather replies. "Also an astronomer, lawyer, and congressman. He was a genius, truth to tell. Built an astronomical clock in 1790 that still keeps perfect time, and no one has been able to reproduce it. One of his relatives, Abaiah Folger, was Benjamin Franklin's mother."

I smile, thinking of old Ben's great-niece, the one who once lived in my home.

"Mmm," Phee says, fiddling with her sneaker lace. "But why does Walter Folger keep popping into my head? I can't concentrate. It's like he wants me to *do* something."

Sal, never one to be surprised at the way the past dies slowly on his island—if at all—glances sideways at his granddaughter.

"Perhaps he wants you to notice something . . ." Sal hesitates.

"Something wrong," Phee suggests, reading his face.

She feels a sharp tap on the shoulder, but it isn't her grandfather. He's across the room.

"Something *heartless,*" she blurts. The words pop out as if someone else had said them. Even Phee looks surprised.

"Exactly. An injustice." Sal's mouth is a grim line.

~

Phee has this on her mind the next day as she meets with the Gang.

I have it on my mind as well.

"Hurry up, you guys!" Phee calls as she trots ahead.

What's left of Mrs. Lyon's home is still quiet a day later, as Eddy has been unable to coax the crew to return. The kids know better than to count this as a victory, but it's a pause.

They decide to head toward their next house, which is at the end of Pine Street. The kids know it's one of Eddy's prime projects. He recently bought the place for nothing, and few improvements have been made in the last half century. He claims a gut job is the only remedy.

The Gang lines up across the street. A worker marches around the side of the house with a sign he pounds into the front garden: *Nold, not Mold! Call Eddy and enjoy a flavor of Old with the best of New!*

"Pah," Phee says and spits in the dirt.

Gabe squints at a first-floor window. "Hold on," he says.

First, a plump little hand flattens itself on the glass. Next, the face of an older kid, a girl who grins with no front teeth, then a serious boy with freckles. Now a head bounces into view, then vanishes. *Bonk, bonk!* Here, now gone. Gabe realizes that the kid is jumping, leaping up to catch glimpses of him.

The three have curly hair and sunburned skin. "See them?" he breathes. No one else does.

Now Gabe steps quietly toward the front door.

Eddy Nold's voice drifts around the side of the building.

"Come on," Phee whispers to the others. "Let's distract Eddy and his crew while Gabe's inside."

The Gang hurry behind the house and gather by a huge dumpster. Paul leans on the side. To their surprise, the crew and contractor ignore them.

Suddenly, Gabe's face appears upstairs and he gives a thumbs-up sign to his friends.

As the Nold crew step toward the back door, hammers and saws in hand, Phee squeals.

"Quick!" She grabs a stone and hurls it toward the rear wall. *Whang!* It thumps on the shingles. As soon as the adults turn, the kids freeze. The crew look back at the house and another stone flies.

And then something else takes over. As the Gang watch, mouths open, stones pelt the back of the building, rolling down the roof and bouncing off drainpipes and framing. The workers back away in a stumbly group, and the Gang stand quietly to one side, trying not to smile.

"What a pity," Maria says loudly.

"A mystery," Markus adds.

Now Eddy Nold, as if not wanting to look cowardly, steps boldly toward the house, a clipboard shielding his face. Stones thump on the back of his jacket, his work boots, and his legs. "Ow," he mutters as the back door swings closed behind him.

Outside, no one moves.

Suddenly a man-sized shout: "Yeooow!" The handle to the door rattles and turns, but it doesn't open. A curtain covering the window in the door ruffles madly, as if there's a struggle inside.

The Gang is surprised that the Nold crew members exchange panicky looks but don't move to help their boss.

It's Cyrus who steps boldly toward the door and flings it open. He then hurries back to the group of kids, and the adults nearby stare at the ground, looking stunned.

Just as Phee says to them, "No worries! He's quick," meaning Cyrus, Eddy flies out the back door. The contractor's feet do not touch the steps.

His arms are spread at a weird angle like wings. He lands on one knee and then, with a groan, tips slowly onto his face.

As the crew help him to his truck, the Gang hear Eddy mutter, "Little fingers. Pinching! Nose, ears, neck—every bit of bare skin. Not wasps, no people inside. Impossible!"

The kids shrug quietly to each other as the last of the workers leave the site. Looking up at the second floor, they spot Gabe zipping by one window and then another, followed by three unfamiliar heads of hair.

"There he is!"

"Ohhh! Plus three ghosts!" The exclamations flow. The Gang sees the same thing I do, but . . . they don't see me.

The four are moving fast.

Phee's face is now hard to read. I imagine she's wondering if Gabe joined the ghosts in attacking Eddy Nold. Who is leading whom?

I wonder, too. Gabe's never been a mean or rough kid—was he forced to do it? Or is he being chased by the same group that went after Eddy? By kids who are now confused and think this boy who walked inside might be a bad guy, like the contractor?

Phee must be thinking the same thing. Her voice quavers as she calls out, "Gabe?"

Soon there's a chorus of nervous voices shouting to Gabe from outside.

No answer.

The kids in the Gang exchange glances and, moving shoulder to shoulder, step inside. The house smells sad. Sad and bad.

Phee rushes to the bottom of the stairs, calling, "You okay?"

"Be right down," Gabe gasps, clearly out of breath. "Stay there."

Eyes are wide as the Gang follows the overhead running. *Bam, bam, bam, bump!* Small feet dash back and forth, bodies bouncing wildly off walls as if they're playing a game of tag.

"Can we help?" Maria calls up. "We saw them. I mean, their heads!"

No answer, but sounds of—what? Murmuring? Mice in the walls?

"GABE PINKHAM!" Phee cups her hands around her mouth. Then she slaps her ear with one hand, her neck with the other, squealing, "Quit it! Cut it out!"

Flinging open the door, she rushes back outside, the rest of the Gang after her.

"Holy moly," Markus pants. "Not nice."

"GABE!" Phee shouts at the top of her lungs from outside. "I'm calling your dad if you don't come out NOW!"

A moment later, Gabe bursts outside and collapses in a pile. "Whew, this is harder than I thought," he gasps. "Wait—catch my breath—tell you in a minute—"

As soon as he's able, they start back toward the Old North Cemetery. No one speaks until Gabe is ready.

"When I'm with some of these ghost kids, it's like I suddenly have to do what they want me to do. In Lydia Lyon's house, they moved me into a corner and showed me all those scenes from the past. In this one, they want more.

I wasn't doing any *pinching*, but I was running. Those kids are ready to fight, like they know what's happening to their home. They're rough. I think it's obvious I'm useful and on their side, but you guys should stay clear. You okay, Phee? And . . . this creeps me out a bit . . ." Gabe pauses. "There are older ghosts around, and they seem to be *guarding* the kids. Peering out of doorways and in windows. Watching and waiting."

"You mean they were *out here* with us while you were *inside*?" Paul asks.

"Think so. Some of them."

Phee remembers Sal's stories of family ghosts who look out for kids and glances at the other members of the Gang.

"Who do you think threw all those other stones?" she asks, sounding braver than she feels. "It's a good thing they did. If we hadn't shown up and Gabe had gone inside with the ghost kids, all those stones might not have been thrown, Eddy Nold might not have been scared off, and the crew might have done a whole lot of damage today."

"I'm the baitfish that draws in the bigger fishes," Gabe announces, puffing his chest out. "The ones that really bite."

No one disagrees. Phee pats her friend's shoulder. "You okay with that, Mr. Pufferfish?"

He shrugs and grins. "Why not?"

Despite his bold words, the Gang speed up, each imagining the *whoosh* of something big slipping along in the deepwater shadows behind them.

CHAPTER 16

A nail, some maps, a run at dusk

November 17.

The day after the Pine Street visit, Gabe wakes with a headache and sore throat.

"You're staying home today, son," his mom announces, handing him a mug of tea with lemon and honey.

Gabe nods happily and wriggles deeper under the covers. Although he was fired up yesterday, he's relieved to have a quiet day in his pajamas.

Eddy Nold feels unwell and his bruises hurt. He stays on the couch. Town is a quieter place.

At the Folger house, the mysterious pile of old boards has become a mountain, spilling clear across the back porch and covering parts of windows.

Sal snaps his suspenders and scratches his chin.

He peers closely at the muddy ground. Yep, there are footprints all right, and they aren't his or Phee's.

"But how?" he murmurs aloud.

"I think it's the boards wanting to be here with us," Phee says cheerfully, as if that explains everything.

After his granddaughter leaves for school that morning, Sal sets off to visit each of the construction sites around town. He wants to chat with the workers, at least those who speak English, but can't seem to find anyone with time to talk.

Every site has a large dumpster. Sal peers inside one after another. "Wasteful," he mutters to himself. "Sinful," he adds, noting hand-turned balusters and the swirl of a newel-post.

One of Sal's relatives, a real estate agent, was recently overheard saying to a friend, "White sells. Real old is *old*, it pulls things down. The more like Palm Beach you can be, the bigger the sale price. Put in a white kitchen and foyer, add a coupla marble bathrooms, open up those cramped little rooms, turn up the lights, haul everything to the dump but a wall joist or two, put up a quarter board with the original date of the building, and you'll be a rich man. People pay top dollar for historic that isn't."

Never one to pick fights with family, Sal only grunted when he'd heard this. Everyone knows that kitchens and bathrooms need to be replaced over time, but not the entire interior of an old Nantucket house.

At site after site, he sees workers using mostly unseasoned wood and drywall. When Sal peers in windows, he finds little true restoration. Sometimes the new interior construction mimics a part of the traditional Quaker design or layout, but it does not feel the same.

Sal now asks why they've ripped out old lumber that's still good, wanting to hear the reply. He is answered with a cold shoulder.

Rudely, the workers act as though he hasn't said a thing.

Straightening his sock hat, Sal picks up a handmade nail lying in the dirt and turns it over in his hand. Made a couple of centuries ago by an island blacksmith, it is one of a kind and still strong.

If only the old wood and iron could rise up and defend itself, he thinks with a wry smile.

The people who built these houses would like that. Most worked hard to make ends meet, and when they built a house to live in, rarely refused an uneven board. They used decking from old whaling ships and even the pickled planks salvaged from shipwrecks, patching them in at the turn of a stairwell or the edge of a room. They hated waste.

Waste, waste. As he turns away, the word circles around and around. *But what if* . . . Sal stops midstride, almost colliding with a worker who stares at him, or rather, at the hand holding the nail.

Startled, Sal shrugs and drops it. Did the man think Sal was *stealing*? The worker watches the nail fall, eyes wide as if there were something dangerous about that little piece of iron.

"Handmade. Long time ago," Sal says to the man, but there is no response.

Really! Sal thinks to himself as he trudges away. Odd.

Looking back, he sees the man pick up the rusty nail as if it might attack him.

~

When Phee comes home that afternoon, the kitchen table is covered with tattered maps of the island and Sal looks excited.

"There's the Southeast Quarter, out Tom Nevers way. This chunk by the shore was taken over by the government during the Cold War years, became a navy base, and is now back under town ownership. Used only for overflow sports and that county fair each year, got a few old buildings and lots of weeds. Trouble with erosion on the south, along the ocean, but on the north . . ." Sal's voice trails off. "A few empty acres there. The question is, will anyone object?"

"Sal?" Phee is lost.

Her grandfather rubs his hands together. "You know the wood that keeps appearing out back. Well, Nantucket Hands can build with what they've left. We need a piece of forgotten land, and guess what: This *is* one."

"Excellent!" Phee gives Sal a quick hug and bounces from one foot to the other, causing the floorboards to creak.

"Quit flopping around like a fish out of water unless you want to get your great-grandmother mad." Sal looks anything but angry. "She hated when your mother crashed around inside, and once threw a wooden soup ladle at her. Flew right across the kitchen on its own and whacked her on the bottom." He leans back and laces his fingers behind his head.

Like it! I can see Phee thinking to herself. *Family. People who never leave each other.*

At that moment, Phee feels a kind of *whoosh,* as if she were on a swing. She takes a step toward the kitchen door.

That's it! She can hardly wait to get going.

Sal is looking at the map now and doesn't see her face. He straightens his sock hat, and wiry white hair spouts like steam from a hole on the side. "We could encourage a few working people to take this pile of ours and just start building."

"Terrific." Phee nods. "Be right back."

She and her grandfather are so close that she rarely hides anything, but suddenly she needs a moment alone.

Sal raises an absentminded hand.

As Phee hurries down one street and up another, she thinks about the old Nantucket names that have been floating into kids' minds, the wood drifting invisibly across the Folger yard, and now Sal's idea about land.

What was it that pushed her away from home just now, as if to give her a chance to sort things out?

Suddenly she's filled with thoughts of her mom. She and Sal had written to her about the Nantucket Hands idea, but haven't heard back. Is she as fierce as Flossie? What would her mom make of the Old North Gang's adventures? And what about that strange word that popped into her mind the other day?

Heartless.

Phee shivers and glances around. Is something or someone trying to reach her? Is her mom or Sal in danger?

Realizing how alone she is at that moment, she gulps. I gulp, too.

I'm tempted to ring my bell, but when you call out *danger,* it's best to know what the danger is.

Dusk comes early in November. As the shadows of rooftops and trees lace fingers across the road, Phee wonders what her life would be like if her mom had never left.

A longing sends her rocketing back toward home, comforted by the sudden thought that Flossie might be on the steps to the kitchen right *now,* back from all those years away. Maybe *that* was the hope that sent her off on her own, the dream of finding her mom waiting when she returned.

Flossie, back with a full heart! Ready to help her daughter and father. The thought makes Phee bold as her feet pound through the empty streets of town.

Heartless, the ice-blue shadows seem to whisper. *Heartless.*

Sal notices that whenever he turns his back, the maps on his table rearrange themselves as if another person is working, too. Someone strong-minded.

When Phee bursts back in the kitchen door and looks around as if expecting to see someone else, Sal is startled.

"What?" he asks his granddaughter.

"Nothing," she replies quickly, but her voice is disappointed.

Sal's face is thoughtful. Knowing there's comfort in a question, he says, "I've been wondering *why us,*" he says. "Why *our* yard? Whoever is bringing the lumber could have chosen a much more public spot and gotten the whole town to notice."

"It's odd," Phee agrees.

If you ask me, I think the recent pileup of old wood in their yard has something to do with how Sal and Phee use the town dump. The way they assume that almost everything in life can be reused or shared. All natives, ghosts perhaps most of all, understand the Folger yard. They can read it like a book.

Phee and her grandfather dress almost entirely from the Take It or Leave It shed at the dump, as it's called. It's halfway to Madaket, at the west end of the island, and is actually a recycling center plus a landfill.

They each have a large backpack, of course found there: Both are orange. "The color of survival," Sal remarks.

"Or tangerines, pumpkins, the bill of an oystercatcher, the sunset—" Phee grins.

"Smarty-pants." Her grandfather gives her a little shove and she shoves him back.

Several times a week they go to the dump to pick through the piles. Pants, shirts, sweatshirts, even sneakers; once Phee saw a young woman unearth a beautiful wedding dress and weep with joy, taking it as a sign that, yes, she should marry her boyfriend. Sal and Phee have also found all of their blankets, sheets, and a ton of books.

Sal will browse through piles of gear and tools while Phee does the clothes shopping for them both. Some days it's sparse pickings. Other days—and most weekends—it's a spread.

Partly because it's difficult to get things off Nantucket and in part because islanders have always been thrifty folk, belongings tend to float around and around in circles. Perfectly good sofas, curtains, rugs, and tables appear at the Take It or Leave It, creating ripples of delight and even the occasional fight. Finding a treasure at the dump is something to talk about, and furnishing a house from the dump is a badge of distinction. It's been done countless times.

In my day, people tossed only empty bottles and broken plates, or perhaps insect-eaten wood. Much of it tumbled down steep banks or into marshes. Places no one wanted to go. I would have loved this town dump. It's like a birthday every day of the year, although it can get rough.

Phee once got knocked flat by two women having a push-me-pull-you over a new feather comforter. Sal got a black eye when a man carrying a lamp spun around to grab another, decking him with a spiky brass pineapple.

No one intends such injuries. They are simply known as Dump Bumps. For those who enjoy diving into the piles, it's a bit like the hazards and pleasures of bodysurfing on a windy day. Scraped elbow? Didn't get to the unopened box of dishes in time? Missed the crest of a perfect wave? Not to worry—there will be other tides and Saturdays.

Nantucket's spirit, after all, has always belonged to the frugal. Also, to those who understand that no one who has lived on Nantucket is ever quite done with it, no matter how many years they've been off in the world, hunting, harpooning, and perhaps hanging on to some rope or job for dear life.

I see all kinds of fishing on this small island, in addition to the kind at the dump.

Witness those—like me!—who are no longer alive but busier than they were when breathing. Someone with a hook is piling those boards in Sal's yard, but the question is, who?

And what are they trying to catch?

CHAPTER 17

An unmistakable scent

November 20.

Eddy Nold is feeling better. He's also losing patience with the craziness going on at his work sites.

At Lydia Lyon's house today, the front door—white pine with a wooden latch and an ivory acorn for a handle—was gently removed by workers. The new owners want a heavy mahogany door in its place. Instantly, every original window or door left in the house opened and closed for a full half hour, the old wood slamming and rattling on its own.

Whang! Bam! Crash! People driving by heard the noise and saw workers leaping away from the building. There was nothing Eddy could say to keep them there. It wasn't until the property was emptied of people that the banging stopped.

Eddy stands outside this afternoon and looks up at the second floor. He kicks some soda cans under a bush and walks across the torn-up yard toward my house. He steps over the back fence, tromps angrily across the yard, and heads for my front door, feeling in his pocket for a key.

Aieeeeee! I panic and scream, "Hey! He's *coming*! Heeeeeeelp!" Jagged sound floats out over the blue afternoon light, but does anyone hear me? The Old North Gang—where are they? I'm not sure what I should do, aside from these words, my horn, and my bell.

Here's hope: still no wind. All can be heard.

Before Eddy reaches my front door, I leaf quickly through Nantucket's past, noticing weapons. I never thought of myself as ferocious when living, but now that my home and others like it are in mortal danger, I find myself thinking of knives and sticks and harpoons in a new light.

I also wonder who we islanders really are. Perhaps more of us are bad than good.

Let's look back.

There was the Wampanoag Indian tribe, who named Nantucket after Maushop kicked off his second slipper, long before the first English settlers hopped off a boat in 1659. Sadly, thousands of welcoming Native Americans were killed off in a short time by European diseases.

Another piece of ugliness involves the whaling industry. Forgive me if you already know, but a whale is the largest of intelligent mammals and not a cold-blooded fish. It can be caring, sad, or angry, and can watch you with a very human eye the size of a grapefruit, an eye that blinks. Whales sing. They care for their young.

Killing a whale is not like killing an eel.

The European settlers took this brutal hunt, first practiced close to shore by the Wampanoag, to a new level in wooden ships that sailed across oceans. By the 1840s, Nantucket had built the largest whaling empire in the United States. This tiny island's name was known around the world.

At its height, this community boasted a town of ten thousand residents and many industries. A Town Crier walked the streets come rain or shine, making enough noise to raise the dead.

As in any boomtown, there was crime. We had hangings and murders.

Weapons were everywhere. Knives, axes, saws, lances, harpoons, and scythes were as common as spoons and forks.

Those who went out on the ships were often gone for years at a time as these compact floating factories sailed around the world. When a whale was chased, harpooned, and killed, the crew worked night and day. Every job was dangerous, truly the stuff of nightmares. Certainly the process of leaping into a small rowboat, stabbing one of those majestic creatures, and then being violently dragged along—a Nantucket sleigh ride!—as a witness to its painful death, if not your shipmate's or your own; the swirl of sharks attracted by the gore; the endless cutting and boiling down of the blubber in order to make oil; the process of removing buckets of coveted spermaceti oil from the huge head—often by climbing inside it and slithering around, a funhouse horror—and just plain surviving days of black smoke and decks slippery with blood and fat. Crew members who weren't hurt during the chase were sometimes mortally injured while handling greasy, razor-sharp cutters and sliding in ankle-deep goo. The end result, amazingly, was many neatly sealed barrels of oil, stored belowdecks until they were unloaded on a Nantucket wharf. It was an ugly, smelly, exhausting job for the men, and cleaning the ship and themselves after each whale must have felt close to unbearable.

Perhaps because of this violent profession, whaling crews were also the ones who taught themselves to make exquisite scrimshaw while on board, spending weeks carving and etching intricate images on a whale's tooth or hunk of bone. Seamen created art that is now in museums. Meanwhile, the women left behind had become literate and business-savvy members of the workforce.

The men weren't the only ones bred to survive.

We were famous during the whaling days for our independent women. Lucretia Coffin Mott, Phebe Coffin Hanaford, and later, Maria Mitchell—these were people who fought publicly for human rights at a time when few spoke out. In part because of them, the great Frederick Douglass gave his first speech to a mixed-race audience at the Atheneum library, in our town.

When the whaling economy of Nantucket crashed, it happened fast. The Great Fire of 1846 destroyed most of the downtown businesses just as kerosene, cheap and plentiful, phased out whale oil for lighting.

It was a terrible one-two blow.

The island plunged into a deep depression, and thousands of our young people left. Sadly, there wasn't enough work to go around, not anymore. Many headed for the Gold Rush in California.

Tourism brought the island a trickle of money by the end of the century, as did a summer actors' colony and a growing number of visiting painters and writers. The good side of those scrape-bucket decades was that this Quaker town survived intact, frozen in time. There was little money to build, and those who remained could only patch and repair.

I have an idea! Perhaps *that* is when the ghosts first took charge, settling deep into the weathered wood and deserted streets of their familiar home. And did those ghosts, men and women as tough as boot leather, *teach* those who came after?

How obvious this is! The world-famous determination that fueled Nantucket's whaling days didn't just disappear. Why would it?

That fierceness is a part of the fabric of every old house. For decades these houses weren't threatened, so no ghosts had to rise to defend their territory.

I'm dizzy at the thought! *Do ghosts like ours see children as apprentices?* Useful, fresh young hands who can be put to work?

When I was a young girl, ghosts were an everyday part of our lives and certainly of our homes. There was nothing shocking about a visit.

There were times my parents and I heard a sharp rapping in the hall at the top of the stairs when we were downstairs at night. My mother would call up, "Bringing a light, Aunt Sally," and the sound would stop. When the family went to bed, we'd set an extra candle, a sturdy one with a glass globe to protect it from drafts, at the top of the stairs. We left it burning. I never thought it was odd. My mother explained to me that her aunt, an avid gardener, had fallen and broken a leg as an older woman, and claimed it was because her candle had gone out. After the accident, she had to sit on a footstool while weeding, and it made her furious.

The morning after the rapping, my mother would find something fresh lying on the kitchen table, such as a handful of basil, a juicy tomato, or some lovely beets. She'd then thank Aunt Sally.

Our doors were never locked, but it wasn't a neighbor who left these gifts.

No one had much to give away. That's part of the reason I go on about the free clothing and furniture at the dump. The flow of goods looks ridiculously easy to me, and maybe it is.

Too easy.

Perhaps it is dangerous.

Balance, for those who live by the sea, is essential. Any boat is small and every ocean huge. Islanders have always known about the tipping point. Once you lose your balance, the sea won't wait for you to catch your breath.

It can't. Waves follow waves.

Which brings me to the present and to Eddy Nold, my house key hot in the palm of his hand. Eddy is not the real problem; he handles what's visible. Today, Nantucketers—expert at fishing for centuries now—have hooked some of the wildly rich. If you ask me, these fish are far too big for us. Is it too late to unhook them and hope they swim away?

The whalemen were killers who used *every last bit* of the lives they took. We use all we can reach. Truth to tell, the people demolishing the interiors of old houses these days don't understand how self-sufficient an islander can be.

Eddy pauses by my front door, as if hearing a sound inside. Then he looks around, sniffing. I listen and sniff, too.

I see Eddy's face soften. We both recognize—wait, can this be?—the unmistakable smell of fresh wonders.

The contractor stands back from the front door, a strange expression on his face. Then he and I hear the clink of a plate set down gently inside, on the front hall table.

Otherwise, there's no sign of life. The windows of my house are dark.

Eddy takes two steps back, spins, and runs.

∽

What is a ghost story?

Some say it's a supernormal tale involving people. I like that word better than *paranormal*. *Supernormal* sounds like more than usual. Perhaps it's a pillow filled with feathers instead of rags, or a fat, blueberry-filled biscuit. Like cream instead of skim milk. Like the luxury of gravy instead of nasty, dry meat. Like a lobster sunset instead of a shy blush.

Kids and ghosts have much in common. Both can and do change shape. Both know how to hide.

Children understand the supernormal without even trying. For them, it's like laughing or crying—it just happens.

Ghosts are extra-normal around here.

Does that mean more real than the living?

I think it does.

My hands tremble. I wipe the handle of my bell and clean my horn.

I know I'm not responsible for that plate, nor is Eliza Rebimbas. Is a batch of supernormal wonders a good thing?

CHAPTER 18

Aunt Thankful by the window

November 21.

The Old North Cemetery.

Although his sore throat is gone, Gabe's voice is squeakier than usual.

"I got news," he says, looking around at the other members of the Gang. It's the day after Eddy paused at the door of my home, before Phee can share Sal's plan to use that mysteriously growing pile of old lumber.

"My dad told me that, starting last night, *every single* 'renovation' site in town is in trouble," Gabe hurries on. "Those big earthmoving machines are breaking down. All of the equipment that helps a worker pull apart the tight joints of an old house—hammers, saws, crowbars—is being scattered. Tossed out, thrown in mud puddles, ruined. And then someone's completely emptying the dumpsters at night, not just taking a board or two."

"Oh, wow," Phee mutters.

"What if people think your grandpa's doing it?" Cyrus asks.

"Herbie's already worried about that." Phee glances at Gabe.

"Yeah, everyone knows that Sal Folger hates the house-gutting." Gabe chews on a thumbnail. "But he's one kinda old guy, I mean . . ."

"Ridiculous." Phee nods. She wonders, suddenly, what Sal's been up to lately while she's at school.

"Hey, you know the names in our heads?" Paul looks around at the group. "What if they're *here*? Maybe some of the old house owners with those names are buried right around us, in this graveyard, and they've been *listening*."

"Watching us," Markus adds.

Even Phee looks shaken by that idea, her mouth rounding down like the top of an old gravestone. "Like right now?" she asks.

"*I* listen," Maddie says promptly. "To people when they tell secrets."

Paul pokes his little sister and she squeals. "Like *you've* heard any secrets," he says to her, and she sticks out her tongue, then hugs him.

"What if some of *them* know some of *us*," Maria says slowly. "And they don't want us talking?"

"You mean, the 'some of us' who are out here playing all the time," Markus says. "Maybe they think *we* live out here, too."

"Ooh." Cyrus hugs his knees.

The kids glance around at the rows of lichen-covered stones on all sides. Smoky greens, slate blues, grays, and marbled creams trade color with the wintery clouds overhead. In certain lights, stone and sky can seem like cousins.

"Look," Phee says. "All of us here have relatives buried on the island, right? So . . . like Sal says, family is family. They'd never hurt us, no matter how angry they are."

"Yeah, Grandma Sue says that, too," Cyrus mutters.

Gabe elbows Phee. "Look, right over there, *Elizabeth Folger*, died in 1844."

"Oh! Right," Phee says, hiding a shiver. "Anyway, hey, speaking of family." She points to a *Tristram Pinkham* nearby. "Died in 1853."

Gabe swallows. "So we all belong," he says loudly, as if to be sure the stones hear.

"I've been thinking," Paul says. "If these are spirits protecting their old houses, they're being kind of hard on the living workers. That doesn't make sense. If they were plain old Nantucketers, they were probably workers themselves."

"Eddy's getting hurt worse and worse," Gabe says. "I know he asked for it, but . . ."

I remember with fear the word that flew into Phee's head a few days ago when she ran out into the dusk, thinking of her mother.

Heartless.

"When people—or maybe ghosts—get desperate, they can forget what's right and do weird things," Phee says. In a flash, she thought of her young parents leaving her alone at night on a leaky boat in the harbor.

Sometimes caring can't stop bad things from happening, she thinks.

"How about we *all* go into the next house, not just Gabe." Paul seems to read Phee's mind.

"Stick together." Phee nods. "Join hands."

I grip my bell. The kids don't know about Mrs. Rebimbas's recent words, *Remember to join hands.* Nor do they realize what scared Eddy away from her front door yesterday.

But Mrs. Rebimbas is still alive, I think. *She was nowhere near our house. Who filled that plate yesterday? Not me.*

As if reading my mind, Grandma Sue calls out, her voice warbling across the dark cemetery, "Who wants a WON-DER?"

The kids in the Gang scramble to their feet and race for her kitchen door. I follow.

ᔕ

Maddie stays with Grandma Sue while the other kids head for a work site on Union Street. *No, please!* It's my aunt Thankful's place, a house built in 1802.

Although it wasn't a happy home to me as a child, the sight of it now is wrenching. The interior has been torn apart, and I mean *torn*. Peeking in from the street, we see old lumber and plaster tossed into crude piles around the bones of new rooms.

Phee and I both imagine how the house must be weeping. The old front door leans at an angle against the foundation, its cast-iron thumb latch looking like a tongue longing for water. A fresh door with shiny modern hardware has just been installed, and the chrome glints with an unnatural brightness in the low afternoon light, drawing all eyes.

"It looks cruel." Phee voices the others' thoughts.

"Hey, there's the name of the guy who built the house, on that old Historical Association plaque." Maria points.

Markus reads it first. "Charles Wyer. Anyone recognize it?"

I do, I shout. *My middle name is Wyer!* But the kids don't hear me.

Phee shrugs. "Could be that the names in our heads belong to the longest owners of these houses, not necessarily the folks who built them." She pauses. "Names in our town are flowing like—" She stops, surprised at her own words.

"—blood from a wound," Gabe finishes, as if reading her mind.

The words shock, but then two workers hurry around the side of the house carrying a table saw. One has blood running down his arm. Without looking up, they head straight for Gabe.

Jumping out of the way, he asks, "You guys okay? Can we help?"

The men speak to each other in rapid-fire Spanish. One hesitates, looking at the kids, as Eddy roars around the side of the house, shouting, "Cover it and let's get going! Need to get these injuries checked at the hospital." Holding one shoulder, the contractor grimaces and waves a floppy arm as more workers stumble out, one holding the side of his head, another clutching his side. Everyone piles into a nearby van. It careens out of sight.

Silence settles on an empty Union Street. The kids look up at the house. The windows gaze back, as if asking for help.

The roof is partly off, like a wig that has slipped to one side. Wooden shutters hang at sad angles. Between them, a row of expressionless new windows still have manufacturing stickers. A tattered needlework pillow props open the last of the very old casement windows, a narrow one with many panes and glass as rich with shimmer as a summer tide pool.

The kids notice it and feel sad.

"Not right," Maria says.

"Some say old glass is liquid, you know," Paul adds thoughtfully. "A really slow liquid. Just learned that in science class this year. Like it looks solid and unchanging but really isn't. Although our teacher said it might not be true, experts don't agree."

"Our house is kind of like that," Phee blurts. "It's always making creaks. Looks not-alive, but really is. We think." She then looks embarrassed.

"You got *real* ghosts?" Cyrus asks.

Phee shrugs. "Maybe," she says, not wanting to scare her friends away from coming over when Sal isn't there. "Don't you?"

Before anyone can reply, she adds quickly, "Come on, let's peek inside. We're alone now."

"Maybe," Cyrus murmurs.

Phee smiles at him. "Glad you get it," she says cheerfully, and stepping over my millstone, marches toward the kitchen door around the back.

Inside, tools are scattered. A can of lavender paint has tipped on its side, the spill still glistening. "Watch your step," Gabe cautions. "My dad would be upset if he knew we were in here after—well, the accidents," he adds, sounding as though *he* isn't too happy about it, either.

"Look," Maria says tenderly. "Poor house!" She points to a wall that is half gone. Plaster and old lathe are thrown in a corner, leaving a gaping hole into the next room. A part that's still intact has faded wallpaper patterned in tiny red roses and one bright rectangle where a picture had hung, probably for decades.

I catch my breath. The ugliness of it all . . . I know what should be hanging in that spot. My aunt Thankful told me it was a picture of her.

"Oh! And here it is!" Markus picks a small painting out of a nearby trash can. The glass is broken but the watercolor inside the frame looks perfect. I don't have to look—I know it depicts the section of Main Street with Phee's house on it, a horse and carriage drawn up in front.

Knowing how interwoven the island's families are, this has never surprised me.

"Here you go." Markus grins, handing it to Phee.

She smiles, looking as though it's the best gift ever. "Thanks—great find!"

"It's a sign." Gabe nods, peering closer. "And look, there's a lady with a bonnet in your upstairs window."

They all peer at the painting, noticing first one thing and then another. A Boston terrier sits on the freshly painted front steps. Pink and purple hollyhocks grow where there are now only weeds and old barrels.

"Huh," Phee muses. "I wonder which Folger that is upstairs. She looks so hopeful and happy."

Not a Folger, I think to myself. *A Wyer! And she wasn't happy when I knew her.*

Just then the back door claps shut, as if the house doesn't want the picture to go.

The kids instinctively move closer to each other, grabbing for each other's hands. Markus leans the picture against a wall.

Phee clears her throat. "Sorry, house. I should have asked. I'm Phoebe Folger Antoine. I live inside the home in your picture, and my family always has. Can I take this and keep it safe? I promise I'll hang it right up."

The door blows back open, and a yellow-handled screwdriver rolls across the floor, stopping in front of the group. The kids stand quietly for a moment, looking at it.

"I think that's a yes . . . and maybe the house wants us to replace the old front door before we go," Paul suggests.

They do just that, carrying it gently back up the steps and propping it in place as the hinges are torn. The new door is easy to remove and they lean it against the dumpster, next to the road.

"Maybe someone building a new home can use it." Phee looks pleased.

"Bye, house," Maria says gently, patting the shingles.

Phee adds, "Thanks again for the painting, and don't worry." She presses a hand to her mouth and then holds it up toward the roof, as if to send a kiss.

"We're rooting for you," Gabe promises.

"Yeah," the others mumble. "We are, we are."

"Grandma Sue must be looking for us by now," Cyrus announces, as if to let the house know they have a reason to leave.

Phee picks up the painting, but feels suddenly dizzy. She puts it down again.

"Something is wrong," she mumbles, still studying the image. "Oh!" she exclaims. "I'll bet I know who that is!"

"So do I," I say, but I don't think they hear me.

Phee looks around at her friends. "I think this is the woman my grandfather's father, Caleb, wanted to marry but then didn't. She stayed in our house for a while when she was in her teens, while the rest of her family had a sickness. Caleb Folger was a young man and they fell head over heels. An artist living across the way did some paintings of her and our house, and we have one, too. She and Caleb were like Romeo and Juliet, just nuts about each other. And then it all fell apart."

"Why?" Markus asks.

"That's awful!" Maria looks stricken.

"I think Sal said it was something about a drowning. The two of them were supposed to be watching one of the Folger babies one day, but they were really watching each other. The toddler crawled off toward a pond and that was it."

"I guess the Folgers didn't want her around after that," Paul adds.

The Gang is silent for a moment.

My aunt Thankful! I marvel. *Why didn't she tell me?* When I was a girl, she never allowed me near deep water and I always thought it was because she didn't want me to have any fun.

I'll bet she, too, wants the island children watched, I mutter to myself.

The kids in the Gang are leaving. They don't hear my words, and I sink down on a broken footstool in the darkening room.

I feel both sad and relieved. I was grateful to my aunt, but didn't like how small she wanted my world to be. As a child, I couldn't understand why she never let me run around with other kids and always wanted me in the yard. And I wrestled with her sadness, which she wore like a punishment right up to the day she died.

I wish she hadn't kept her story a secret.

"Ohhh," I sigh, feeling tired. I was so pleased to matter, to spread the news as the Crier, but *do* I matter?

Perhaps this crisis wrapped around our old homes is about love. Saving the soul of our deep island one board and one spirit at a time—and making sure more children aren't hurt.

Love and the possibility of making things better, and it's *children* who hold the power. Not their parents. Not this Crier.

The Gang and ghosts! Children spy but also forgive, and perhaps that is why they work so well with those who return.

I look around at the wreckage in this home where I once lived.

Suddenly the room fills with a fishnet of voices, and I'm reminded of how cozy *life* can be. People caring. Keeping one another company. I place a hand on one of the old wall joists, and the space around me vibrates with the clink of spoons and forks, boots scuffing, the rustle of chair seats, a murmur of voices.

Families inside a home, people who weren't alive when I was a child, souls still present in the walls and floors. Layers of relatives, of living and dying and trying, *still here* as long as—

"OH!" I gasp. *Thousands* of people lived in all these houses over the centuries. One, two, three, four, a thousand if you count them together . . . and again, and AGAIN! The *numbers*! If I can wake even *some* of them, get them to join forces with the Gang . . .

Hope fills whatever is left of me, and I ring my bell. Before leaving, I decide to bring the painting of my aunt back to my own home, where it won't be alone.

I wish I had known in life what happened to my aunt as a young woman, and that her unhappiness had nothing to do with me.

As I step over the millstone, I blow my crow a kiss.

CHAPTER 19

Words in the dark

Phee has been dreaming about Flossie.

"Sometimes she rushes and gives me a hug, but sometimes she's so sad," Phee tells Sal the morning after the Union Street visit. "Crying, like she misses us. I'm kinda worried something has happened. What if she *needs* us and we don't know?"

"Nah," Sal says, opening the top of the kitchen stove, tossing in a log, and closing the lid again with a *rattle-clank* that Phee would know anywhere. "Last letter we got, she was really 'crazy-busy,' in her words, doing school projects and moving at the same time. I expect she's on her way back here, and when you've been away from home for a bit, the past rushes to meet you." Sal gives his granddaughter's shoulder a squeeze.

"Like wind," Phee says. "Only there's been none for weeks."

"Maybe that's it. No wind makes for strange dreams." Sal is quiet for a moment. "Nervous about her being back?"

"I dunno." Phee shrugs. "A little. But I want to see her, you know?"

Sal studies his granddaughter's face. "Tell her that you're fine before you go to sleep tonight," he suggests. "Mothers have a way of knowing what's happening even when they don't. They also never stop caring about their kids, no matter how old those babies are. I know mine didn't."

"Yeah," Phee says. "Babies!" She pokes Sal, and he pokes her back.

"I'll tell her to quit fussing," she adds.

~

That night before falling asleep, Phee speaks to her mom.

"Flossie—I mean, Mom—it's been so long, and Sal always calls you by your name. Don't worry, I'm doing great and we want you to come home."

She lies quietly, listening to the house creak and a log settling downstairs in the fire. "Mom? I'm still your big girl, and I'm right here."

Suddenly she can hear her mom's voice saying, "You're right here!" just as she used to on the boat when her daughter was little. *Right here, right here . . .* The words echo in Phee's head, but not in a bad way. Sal had known about moms and their kids, that they can communicate sometimes when nobody else knows or hears.

"Right here," Phee whispers. "Right here!"

The knob on her bedroom door turns and the door opens, just enough for a head to peek in. Phee looks up expecting to see Sal, but the hallway is empty. Besides, she's pretty sure Sal is still downstairs reading by the fire. A lemony scent fills her room, a scent she hasn't smelled in years.

"Mom?" she whispers.

There is no answer, but the door closes softly. Seconds later, the door to her mom's old room, the one right next to hers, opens and then clicks shut.

Through the wall, she hears the long-ago, happy sound of her mom humming.

Somehow it all feels right and good, and Phee sleeps like a baby.

CHAPTER 20

Under attack

November 22.

Eddy Nold has had a serious car accident.

He drove into a telephone pole on Union Street. Bones are broken and he looks pretty bad, but he isn't dead.

Although he doesn't know I'm there, I visit him in the Nantucket Cottage Hospital. Here's what I see:

Officer Herbie Pinkham is in a chair next to his bed. "Eddy," the policeman whispers. "What happened?"

Eddy's eyes roll open. Slowly, as if the lids are broken window shades or perhaps belong to a dying sea creature.

"Leaving late. All alone. Swerved away from a bunch of people," he mutters. "Shadowy, but ran right in front of my truck like they saw it. Couldn't just hit 'em . . . Turned the wheel . . ." His eyes slide shut again, and the monitor by his head begins beeping.

The officer leaves, wondering who set a trap for Eddy.

~

The island is in an uproar. Herbie has gotten into the habit of chewing on the inside of one cheek these days. He then grinds his teeth at night. His mouth is a mess.

Although Eddy has more business than any other contractor, there are a few others with "renovation" jobs who plan to gut, not just restore. The crews at these sites are spooked, understandably so.

While Herbie is visiting Eddy at the hospital, a hammer hurtles through the air in one of these houses, whacking a new owner who's paying a visit. He spins around and grabs the worker closest to him, accusing him of an attack.

After he has this innocent man arrested, every other member of that crew walks off the job. Just down the street, buckets of black paint for window trim, neatly lined up on second-story scaffolding, suddenly sprout leaks and pour down the white clapboard front of a newly gutted nineteenth-century home. Paint for the interior, rose and sage and cinnamon, splashes across the walls while the house is empty. A nail gun jumps up and punches holes in several new windows, shooting showers of glass and splintered wood into the street.

Soon every single "renovation" site in town is abandoned.

The police chief calls all of his officers in for a meeting.

The property owners phone their off-island attorneys, although by law these guys will have to work with local police and lawyers to get anything done. The first city attorney arrives at the station in a trench coat and shiny shoes. He has a cashmere scarf knotted around his neck the way they do on Madison Avenue in New York City. He demands to know why the police haven't picked up every worker on his employer's site, which happens to be the one covered in runaway paint.

Just as Herbie approaches the police station, the attorney's scarf is jerked tight as can be around his neck and he's pulled at top speed out the front door.

"Like a disobedient dog," one of the officers on duty remarks later. "One who got into the family garbage can." The attorney collapses in a heap on the sidewalk in front of the station.

Rushing over to him, Herbie crouches by his head. "You okay, mister?" he gasps. He looks around helplessly, but of course can't see a perpetrator anywhere.

The attorney doesn't acknowledge Herbie but now sits up, having loosened the scarf that is strangling him.

"What'm I going to say?" he gasps.

Herbie shrugs sympathetically. There's a moment when the two men seem to share a quiet, respective panic, for it's clear neither can do much.

"Tell 'em it's the ghosts," the officer says.

~

An off-island insurance agent arrives later that same afternoon. This second visitor rents a car at the airport and decides to go directly to the site she's been hired to investigate.

This eighteenth-century house has a STOP WORK sign tacked to the front door.

The property is deserted and looks as though the workers left in a hurry. A table saw has been overturned. Rolls of pink and silver insulation are scattered in the yard. The original windows have been popped out and thrown unkindly against the side of the dumpster. Their watery glass—or what remains of it—twinkles gently in the sun. A pile of old-fashioned ruffly curtains has been used to clean power tools, some of which are still sitting around.

The agent walks slowly up the front steps, careful to keep her suit clean. She has L.L. Bean boots on, which she felt was the only gesture appropriate to this visit; after all, she wants to look like the powerful city businessperson that she is.

The front door is open. She steps inside.

Puddles of water dot the entryway, as well as a scattering of sand and seaweed, as if someone had just stepped off the beach. The woman finds this strange.

There are no witnesses—at least none of the usual kind—so no living person is quite sure what happens next, but I can tell you that I see the woman fly backward out that door as if shoved, rolling and bumping down the steps. She scrambles onto all fours on the sidewalk, crawls a few feet, destroying her suit, and is then *pushed back down* onto her face. By now, her carefully combed hair is a mess and her face is as pasty as uncooked dough.

"Okay! I'm out of here!" she croaks. This time when she gets up, she stays up, and I follow as she limps at top speed back to her car. When she opens the driver's-side door, she is suddenly lifted by the back of her jacket and stuffed into the interior.

She zooms downtown, staggers into the nearest bar, and cleans up in the bathroom. The bartender notices that she has a raw scrape on her chin and is missing a boot.

"Need help, ma'am?" he asks. She shakes her head, busy checking her smashed cell phone for the next flight out.

While driving to the airport, she veers off the road and into a boulder. When Officer Pinkham arrives, it's dusk. The woman is sitting on the rock next to her crumpled rental car. Her teeth chatter.

"People, people w-w-walking." Muttering as if alone, she gestures at the side of the road. "Didn't want to hit them. Came out of the woods, a crowd. L-Long skirts and f-f-funny jackets, old-fashioned, and then . . ." The insurance agent rubs her eyes. "Gotta quit this job. Losing my mind."

The officer frowns. "Me, too" is all he says.

Later that day, Herbie asks his son a few questions.

"So, Gabe. I hear lots of the kids are thinking about old-timey island names. Writin' 'em down, lookin' 'em up. What's going on here? Huh? You guys suddenly turning into historians? Gettin' studious?"

The officer knows his son is always more interested in taking a bike ride than in doing his homework. He is just that kind of kid. Loves being out and about the island—as Herbie had, too, as a boy.

Gabe looks at his dad, head on one side. "Nope. Not interested in old facts, not so much. It's more like—" He pauses, fiddling with the cord on his sweatshirt hood. "—well, like they're using us to do something cool."

The officer swallows. *Using us*, his son said.

Using us.

Herbie is used to thinking his son is a peculiar boy. Not outgoing, a high-pitched voice that could drive you mad, drawn toward spooky stuff and too fearless for his own good. Who in their family—aside from his grandma Hepsa, whom he doesn't remember well—has ever had that dark streak? When they allowed him to pick a dog from the pound to keep him company, he named it Ghost. And truth to tell, the creature looked frightening: gunmetal gray with a fin of hair on his back. He hasn't seen the dog in ages, come to think of it. Oh, yeah—Gabe said the mutt had disappeared one day.

"*Who* is using you?" Herbie Pinkham asks, trying to keep his voice casual. He doesn't like this idea, not one bit.

"The names." Gabe shrugs. "Jonathan Chase. How should I know?" He reaches for his math book and opens it up in the middle, stroking his chin and frowning as if busy, in an adult way. It's a dead giveaway, Herbie thinks to himself. *He looks like he's trying not to tell me any more.*

"Gabe."

"Yeah, Dad?" The officer's son still hasn't looked up.

"Gabe." Herbie Pinkham's voice is now loud. "Look at me. Who's Jonathan Chase? What's going on here?"

Gabe glances at his dad and yawns, covering his mouth to hide the fake gesture. "Holy critters, Dad! It's nothing.

Some guy. Just something fun." Gabe shrugs again. "We middle-school kids like to make up stuff to do, you know? You're always telling me to stay off the computer. Well, that's what I'm doing."

"True," mutters his dad. "Sorry—guess I've had a long day," he says, frowning.

Gabe's heart skips a beat. *Sorry!* Had he ever heard his dad say that word? "That's okay." Gabe pats his dad's shoulder as he slips behind his chair. "Well, I'm off to Phee's house. A bunch of us kids are planning something. Back in time for dinner."

"Huh," the officer says. "Okay."

As his son slams the math book shut and bounces out the front door, Herbie Pinkham can't get those words out of his head.

They're using us to do something cool.

Herbie doesn't like the idea of anyone manipulating his son or any other kids. Who was Jonathan Chase, anyway? Looking at the cover of Gabe's math book, the officer sees that his son has written the name three times under his own name, and in tidy block letters. It looks as though Gabe has gone over and over the lines with his pencil, making them dark and even.

They're using us.

Grabbing for the phone directory, Herbie looks up

the *C*'s, running a big finger down the column. Chase, Chase . . . just as he thought, no Jonathan.

No, the officer decides, thinking of all the violent incidents happening at old houses and the spirits or whatever they've been that traipsed out in front of a truck or appeared from the woods, causing another crack-up . . . No. He doesn't like it one bit.

Ghosts being angry at adults is one thing, but using kids . . .

The officer spills his drink in a fit of nerves, only to realize it must already have run down his front. But no—all is dry. Dabbing at his clean shirt with a sleeve, he looks puzzled.

"Blast the ghosts," he finds himself muttering, then wonders what on earth he's saying. He's taken a vow to protect all people, and on this island that means the haves, have-nots, in-betweens, and all the wash-ashores who come to visit.

Plus everyone else, his grandma Hepsa would remind him.

He fires his can at the garbage and feels better when it hits home.

CHAPTER 21

Where have they been?

The Gang gathers at Phee's house and tempers flare.

"Gabe, I hate to *gally* you, but if you're getting *wadgetty* about being the lure, maybe someone else should do it next time," Phee snaps.

"Don't *muckle* me." Gabe sounds insulted. "You know we can't stand in the yard watching a house surrounded by police! *Or* trespass in front of them."

Meanwhile, Paul and Maria argue about who gets which chair by the fire, and Cyrus and Markus fight about whether the ghosts picked in Ghost Gam might be willing to help out.

Everyone's language is odd, and Phee suddenly laughs and calls out, "Stop, you guys! Listen to us!"

"Yeah," Gabe says, sounding surprised. "What's up with *gally* and *wadgetty* and *muckle*? And how come we kind of understand these weird words? Maybe the ghosts have taken us over and that's why we're so *grouty.*"

"Nah, we've just got a *fair wind* and *everything drawing,*" Phee says, looking startled at her own words.

Gabe's face lights up. "I have an idea! Let's go visit Eddy Nold in the hospital. *Bow on.* He must be in the *mollygrumps.* You know, ask if he's doing okay and find out what he saw on the road."

"You're a wily one, Gabe." Phee grins. "We'll see if he's ready to *come about.*"

Flames lick happily in the fireplace, but Maria shivers. "My parents are worried," she says. "Their friends here are talking. In the Dominican Republic, Haiti, or Jamaica, ghosts don't *whick-whack* around in an innocent way. They say spirits can be *meeching* in bad ways. My mom thinks they can steal kids. Like payback."

Paul shrugs. "But Nantucket is different," he says. "I'll bet the ghosts are friendly, at least to kids like us. They must know we belong to Nantucket Hands. They probably like to spend time going *up scuttle* and *watching the pass,* especially if they're *running before the wind.*"

"Yeah," Maria murmurs. "Like folks anywhere."

"We've made a good start." Phee stretches and yawns.

"All in the course of the voyage," Markus adds. "*Greasy luck to us all.*"

Just then, an empty rocker sitting by the fireplace begins to move. *Creeak, crack! Creeeak!*

Phee reaches out a foot and plops it on the chair rung. "No time for *shooling*," she says loudly, looking at the chair. "The sails are raised and we're all on board. This may be a *slatch* in the storm, but tomorrow we'll *heave ho*."

As if satisfied, the rocker quiets.

~

Something is now worrying me, as the one who announces and warns. Here's what I'm wondering: *Are* Phee, Gabe, and the other kids falling under the spell of ghosts I don't see?

How is that seafaring language easy for them to understand?

And if there are different kinds of ghosts on this island, just as there are different kinds of people in the world, are some of them good and some truly awful?

I was being dramatic when I warned you about the bloody history of this island. It *has* been bloody, but so are most stories about the past.

Humans, after all, are complicated animals. The same behaviors pop up over and over through time: Some beings are kind and sweet, others nasty, and most are a combination. A few are saints, and a handful are killers. The creepiest are the murderers who also smile.

Could there be as many kinds of ghosts around here as there are people? Now, *that* is a scary thought.

Who were the ones coming out of the water, in early November? Or the ones with flickering lights in the graveyard, or the group the Coffin kids saw standing in the snow? And then the shadows that Eddy and later the city people said they could see, causing them to have terrible car accidents . . .

Did these ghosts *target* the kids, the contractor, the attorney, and the insurance agent? Or did they simply cross paths?

Was there a connection, like hooking a fish? Or were the ghosts just drifting, like jellyfish in a tide?

And here's a chilling question: These people, invisible souls leaving their prints on the beach and then in a graveyard . . . WHERE ARE THEY COMING FROM?

Even I, who no longer have blood or feel cold, know the hairs on my head want to rise.

It's true that lots of folks have drowned in the waters around Nantucket. It's happened ever since people lived by the sea, learned to harvest its riches, swam for joy, and then made bigger and bigger boats that floated farther and farther out. It's happened for centuries, and sadly it still happens, despite modern equipment, life jackets, and all the precautions. A moody wave or rogue current, a false step on deck: The sea can snuff out a human just as we crush mosquitoes, simply by reason of size.

I always thought that if that happened to one of us, the water would wash the spirit away, like a fleck of seaweed or an empty clamshell.

If these people all drowned and have come back . . . WHERE HAVE THEY BEEN all this time? Are there souls that live in the waters around this island?

Or have they been near us all this time, and are simply making a ruckus?

I'm worried about who's *at the helm.*

Is it safe to be in the hands of ghosts?

Although I've been one for almost a century, even I don't know.

Do most spirits care when a human being dies? Or is it like someone taking a swim and calling to those on the shore, "Come on in! It's only cold at first!"

I sense mortal danger.

Should I ring and hoot, or is it best to be silent? My heart and mind are spinning.

CHAPTER 22

Thanksgiving dreams and a death

November 23.

"Mr. Nold?" Phee's voice is soft. "Can we ask you a few questions?"

The blinds are down in the hospital room and the sleeping man stirs, adjusting his oxygen mask. His eyes roll open and he gazes at the ceiling.

The Gang gathers around the bed, standing quietly.

"I don't think he can answer, not with that thing on his face," Gabe whispers.

Eddy's hand lifts an inch or two off the sheet, as if to say, *Try me.*

"We could do questions, like with Ghost Gam," Maria suggests.

A worried crease deepens between the contractor's eyes, as if at the word *ghost.*

"I have a better idea," Cyrus says. "Just talk about the old houses. Good stuff. You know, about not hurting them anymore. Then maybe he'll get the idea that making friends with ghosts is a lifesaver."

"Smart," Phee agrees, and Cyrus blushes; a Phee Antoine compliment is rare.

"Maybe then the ghosts won't kill him," Markus adds bluntly.

The group takes turns reminding Eddy of the many ways that Nantucket's heart and soul lives in its old homes. They also tell him about the wishes for housing that are a part of Nantucket Hands. Eddy himself is a longtime renter on the island and would surely appreciate his own place one day.

"So you see"—Paul leans close to the bed—"it's a bad idea to get the island ghosts angry. It's not worth making that extra money, you know? Not if you end up like you are now."

Eddy nods and lifts a hand again, as if to say, *Maybe.*

"And it's almost Thanksgiving," Maria adds. "I know you're not happy to be here in the hospital, but . . . it's a time to be grateful about how much Nantucket gives to all who, umm, *respect* it."

Eddy's eyes are now closed.

The kids tiptoe out.

Behind them, Eddy Nold drifts into the first peaceful sleep he's had since the accident. He has dreams he doesn't forget.

~

November 25.

Gabe and Phee meet at Gabe's house.

"Let's *put out*," Gabe says. "Can't wait for the Town Crier. Too much happening."

Phee nods and both reach for their sneakers. "We'll *scud along* to my place. The others will be there after school."

The Crier! That's not a term many island kids know well, not anymore.

I smile, and then I realize like a splash of freezing water that I've joined the flow of old words in the kids' heads.

Can't wait for the Town Crier, Gabe said.

But am I mostly the Crier, or am I Mary W. Chase?

I fear the Gang may have become louder and stronger than I am, but I am already dead. These children are not.

I hope they sense the strength and anger that seems to be growing in this old town of ours.

Do they understand that we spirits who are here don't always agree?

~

At noon on November 26, Mrs. Rebimbas dies.

She was cheerful and focused this morning. Although alone, she seemed to chat with a visitor seated in an empty chair by her bed. Eyebrows fluttering, she muttered the word *wonders* several times.

"Wonders, Mrs. Rebimbas?" the nurse asked, pleased to see her so lively. "Are you hungry?"

Eliza shook her head. One bony hand lifted in an *I'm busy* gesture. Clearly, she was engaged in an exchange that mattered, but one nobody else could hear or see.

When the nurse returned with a lunch tray, this oldest of Nantucketers was no longer alive.

The doctor stops by to confirm her death. The closest window—a stiff, squeaky old thing—opens slowly on its own, *creeeeeak*, and the first-floor room fills with a pearly, empty-shell light. The curtains stir and twitch, as if pushed eagerly aside by a child climbing out. The doctor, a long-time resident, leaves the room without touching the window. Gently, he shuts the door.

He is moved when he hears of her last word, marveling that this old woman was still thinking about the children in town on her dying day.

A hospital worker immediately says, "Her doughnuts! The best anywhere. She fed so many of us after school.

Always a fresh batch, sugary and warm, sitting on the table inside her door."

When a person passes on Nantucket, the island itself often seems to know. As if there is something elusive in our air, something both cozy and somber that we sense but can't put into words. Those still living don't know what it is but instinctively pull closer to their loved ones.

Before news of her death is out, every doughnut on the island has been eaten. Adults found themselves longing for a treat they hadn't had in years and headed for bakeries and the grocery store. Licking sticky fingers, they smiled about Mrs. Rebimbas and the sweetness of her plate of wonders.

I wish I could still taste.

But what am I saying? This is no time for such longings! With Eliza now gone, my worries for our house loom like a thunderstorm at sea.

CHAPTER 23

Bells gone wild, a red sleeve

After the last doughnut is swallowed, there is a moment of peace and silence before the bells in six of the churches in town begin to chime at once. It's just after three p.m. and not time for any scheduled bell ringing.

What felt at first beautiful and strange soon becomes a cacophony. People cover their ears as the bells jangle and spar, a jarring fabric of sound that continues for a full ten minutes.

Church officials dash to their bell towers, looking for someone to blame.

Even I am shaken. I pause, horn and bell in hand.

I've never heard the church bells in town when they didn't follow each other in a melodious, dignified way. This sounds more like an angry mob, an ugly shouting match pierced by an occasional shriek. When the last chime dies away, frightened voices are everywhere.

"What's going on?" is heard over and over. The police station phones are ringing like mad, speaking of ringing.

I am scared. Should I be ringing, too?

What is the island coming to?

~

Phee and Gabe are halfway to the Folger house when the ringing begins. As the last peal of bells drifts over the treetops, leaving even the skeletal roof walks looking shocked, the two pause by the steps of the Pacific National Bank, the one at the head of Main Street. Oddly, the street is empty.

"What is *that*?" hisses Gabe.

It's a soft shuffling sound, although there's no one nearby.

"It's *people*, people walking," Phee whispers, pulling her friend close to the bank railings. "Quick, hide!"

They duck out of sight behind the outward curve of the old stairwell. An empty wooden bench by the foundation offers a perfect spot and the two scramble beneath it.

"Ouch!" Gabe hits his head just as Phee places a warning hand on his arm.

Something is most definitely coming, and it's coming from all directions.

Everyone who lives on Nantucket knows the uneven sound of walking on an old street or sidewalk. There's a *shushhh-plonk-ka-sleeee-crunk* as any kind of shoe slides on the buried tree roots, slippery stones, worn bricks, and paving blocks.

I, too, hear groups of people, all moving slowly but invisibly toward the two kids—from the Unitarian Church on Orange Street, the Congregational and Methodist churches on Centre Street, the Baptist Church on Summer Street, the Catholic Church on Federal Street, and the Episcopal Church on Fair Street. Converging from the north, south, east, and west. Now the occasional tromp in a puddle, a trip followed by a scuff, the passage of sole after sole on stone.

Phee is the first to peek out. She gasps.

Main Street is empty as the footfalls get louder. People doing errands at the far end of the street are going about their business now that the bells have stopped.

Doesn't anyone else hear this other sound?

Closer . . . *slee-cherp, sleeee . . . sluff-shuffle-nurgle-shuffle.*

"What if they're coming to get us?" Gabe whispers, grabbing Phee's jacket and pulling her toward him.

"Aup!" Phee squawks, not knowing what to think of Gabe so close, the approaching sounds and flash-dash of the moment.

"Maybe it's zombies!" he whispers, and that does it, they're off and running. As they round the corner of the bank, heading full-gallop past the intersection of Fair and Main Streets, Phee's arm smacks something in midair. Something warm and soft.

A *body part*?

She stumbles backward and, in that instant, sees the fastest of glimpses, an image caught in a blink. In that fraction of a second, the surprised face of a woman whirls by, followed by a nip of cranberry-colored sleeve, a wrist, and a hand. An arm raised to protect a face. For a shocked moment, Phee thinks this face belongs to her mother.

To Flossie! Flossie Folger! But Phee knows that's nonsense. Her mom is alive and far away. Behind the startled face, Phee glimpses—or does she?—a group of men and women in old-fashioned clothing, a group moving slowly toward the kids. A knee ruffling a skirt, a boot swinging forward in midstride.

And as fast as she sees and knows all of this, she doesn't.

Gone, *pfft*! Fair Street is empty.

"Gabe," she pants, "I saw them. And dang if they aren't some kind of ghosts!"

CHAPTER 24

An empty teacup, a stolen basket

Gabe and Phee burst into the Folger kitchen.

Paul, Cyrus, Maria, and Markus are already gathered around Sal and his array of maps. As Gabe and Phee take turns spilling a quick version of what just happened, the room becomes dead quiet.

"Like it! Gotta say." Sal places his palms together, then rests them against his mouth. "Did you kids hear about Mrs. Rebimbas's passing today? Maybe it's a welcome parade."

"You're not scared by what I saw, Sal?" Phee asks.

Her grandfather laughs. "*Me* frightened? This island has always had a population of ghosts! They're as common as the fuzz of moss on our shingles or harmless powder beetles in our house beams. Or turtles that cross the road by Maxey Pond to lay eggs, or fog billowing through the streets on a June evening!"

Phee glances shyly at her friends, hoping they won't be startled by her grandfather.

"Mmm," Gabe mutters, pleased but not quite sure. He thinks of his dad's worried face.

Sal now slaps his hands palm-down on the kitchen table, looking from one kid to the other. "Normal it is—at least around here. Phee's heard my stories." He pauses. "I think there are times when our ghost population needs something done, and they show up"—Sal squints at the ceiling for a moment—"to remind anyone who's around to do it."

"What do they want?" Phee prompts him.

Sal leans back. "The way I see this, it's a natural thing. We're all connected. An empty teacup sits in clear sight and so someone fills it. Like water finding its own level."

"*In clear sight.* That sounds creepy, as if ghosts everywhere are watching us," Paul says. He pulls his sweatshirt up over his chin.

Sal's eyes twinkle. "Want to hear about something bad I tried to do when I was about your age?"

He looks around at the group, who nod nervously. "Come to think of it, this is a perfect story for the day. Eliza Rebimbas would be pleased.

"Well, I wanted a basket to give to a girl, but had no way to buy or barter. I snuck to the back of Mrs. Rebimbas's house and into the workroom. Thought I'd help myself to just one piece of perfection out of the many hanging from the beams overhead. All of us kids knew her house, as we'd all ducked in for an after-school wonder, even then. Eliza was out working in the garden, and her husband had gone to check on his lobster pots. I didn't think she'd notice and felt sure that impressing this girl would change my life for the better.

"Now, Eliza's house was old even then, and I'd heard she believed that she and her husband shared it with ghosts. At the time, I didn't think of that. Looking around real quick, I spotted a beauty, reached up, and unhooked it. The basket jumped from my hand, and a flood of salty islander language filled my head. I know I heard someone threatening to 'hang me from the yardarm.' You know, the way a captain killed a mutineer by putting a noose around his neck and dangling him from one of the spars of a ship. I rushed out of there faster than a snake near a rake, and when I looked back, Eliza was smiling. She must've seen the whole thing from the garden, but I'll never know."

For a moment, Sal looks embarrassed. "Didn't get the girl, either."

Phee pokes his knee. "You bad boy, Sal!"

"Bad," he agrees. "But when you need it, I mean when you're trying to come about in a gale or keep your course steady, it does seem like there's help here. It's around us. Sometimes it's a give, sometimes a take. Not like a genie in a bottle, nothing like that; more like the ghosts are around and they want the right things to happen."

"Right for whom?" Gabe asks.

"Ahhh." Sal frowns. "I've never had to be responsible for what an angry spirit can do, like your dad. Never had to explain them to anyone."

Gabe looks uncomfortable. He reties his sneaker, as if that might help.

"It's a tough job. Explaining can get goldarn awkward," Sal says kindly. "And wouldn't you know it, Eliza Rebimbas went out of her way to be generous with me after that basket incident, no doubt knowing that my family didn't have a whole lot to live on. We never said much to each other, Mrs. Rebimbas and I, but she gave me odd jobs around their shop after that, and even sent me home with a basket or two. When her husband died, I made a habit of stopping by to fix anything that needed fixing. That, and keeping her in firewood. Then when my wife, Polly, passed"—and here he glances at Phee—"Eliza took care of Flossie so that I could keep my carpentry jobs.

Always had a soft spot for the kids. Your mom called her Mrs. Bim. I should've taken you to visit her. Don't know where the time has gone." Sal looks at the backs of his hands as if they were to blame.

Phee bounces up, hating to see Sal look mournful. She decides at that moment not *ever* to tell her grandfather that she'd just seen a glimpse of someone who looked like Flossie. He would only worry that something truly *had* happened to his daughter and they'd be unable to check. Sal had already lost too many people he loved.

For some reason, Phee isn't worried. The *right here* exchange from the other night is still with her. She'd *know* if Flossie wasn't fine.

Phee shakes back her hair, now positive that the woman's face might only coincidentally have been like her mom's. After all, so many Nantucketers are related. Distant cousins. And although she remembers her mom wearing a red shirt that was just that color, isn't it logical that in a crowd, one islander might look like another?

"Humph," Phee announces. "Mrs. Bim. Anyone like one of my oatmeal cookies?" she asks, dumping a number of burned disks from a clay jar onto a plate, shapes that look as if they'd emerged from the woodstove months earlier.

No one eats, but all are relieved to change the subject.

As the late-November light peeks through a window, the Gang, plus Sal, come up with a plan.

It will take place at night, with no illumination needed but that of tomorrow's full moon.

Sal sends the kids home then, before their parents notice they've been gone too long.

"No sense in rocking the boat," he says comfortably.

Walking along at twilight, Gabe feels older. Having a run-in with ghosts and then hearing what Sal had to say has made the everyday world look different. The November sky has never felt deeper, the twisty trees have never been more confident, the bumpy streets with their mix of bricks and cobbles never looked truer.

It's as if the pluses fit with the minuses and each footstep matters.

As if there is room for bending the rules of life and death.

CHAPTER 25

Please stay!

A woman sits at dusk on the edge of a bed and knits her fingers together, opening and closing her hands.

"Hey," she whispers. "I'm sorry I left you! So sorry. What is it you want me to do that I'm not doing? I'm here! I'm trying my best."

The room is silent, and the house around the room even quieter.

"Good things . . . moving ahead . . ." Her voice trails off. "Where *are* you? Show me you're here again!"

The words sink into the still November air and the woman sits on, alone.

Soon she sighs and lies down in a ball, curled on her side. *Crack-creeeeak!* A latch clicks and her bedroom door swings slowly open. Hardly daring to breathe, she watches, eyes wide in the gloomy light.

What is *that*? A flash of pitch-black hair and the edge of a cheek that she'd recognize anywhere!

"Yes!" the woman whispers. "*Please* stay!"

CHAPTER 26

Kids by moonlight

That night, young feet creep down sets of stairs and out front doors. Oddly, no parents or grandparents are awake, as if the moon itself has sent them an irresistible dose of heavy, cloudless sleep.

Gabe hurries from his house through the crooked, snoozing streets that lead to the Old North Cemetery. Once there, he spots Cyrus, Paul, and even little Maddie, as well as Maria and Markus. The kids are perched on the split rail fence that borders the road.

After a quick round of whispered *hey*s and a thumb bump from Maddie, they set off at a trot to Phee and Sal's house.

All who have walked this island at night know the gleam of a moonlit, cloudless sky. Perhaps the surrounding ocean reflects and radiates light.

"My heart is jumping," Maria whispered loudly. "It's turned into a frog."

The others laugh and Cyrus says, "Yeah, I'm so awake I can't imagine why we sleep every night. It's awesome out here." He means it, but there is a tremble to his voice. The Gang hugs the shadows at the side of each lane or road, traveling in a line. Everyone is busy imagining whoever carried all of those boards to Sal's backyard, and at night. Strong arms. Many legs. Big feet.

They also think of the footprints seen at the water's edge and in the graveyard.

Meeting up with these ghosts, if that's what they are, is not an easy idea.

Gabe doesn't mention the group of people that Phee glimpsed yesterday—it's too scary to bring that up. Not at night.

He thinks of the shuffling noises—so many shoes!

Maria and Markus remember the firefly flashes at the Old North Cemetery and the crashing sounds that chased them back to their bedroom window.

Maddie, Paul, and Cyrus think separately about the invisible figures collecting snow, and the large bare feet in the graveyard on that same cold night. No one shares what he or she is picturing. All kids know that fear is contagious.

The Gang slips in and out of the pools of deep black that drift beneath the elms.

Paul breaks the silence with a whisper. "I'm thinking about who rescued the wood."

"Yeah," Maddie squeaks. Did the moon make it easier to read one another's minds? "They're doing good." As she says it, she looks up to be sure she's sandwiched between her brothers.

All are quiet for a beat.

"Sometimes, Sal and Phee get restless and step outside on a clear night like tonight," Gabe says softly. "Sal calls it 'taking a lunar.' That's what the retired captains and seamen did; they 'took a lunar reading,' which meant checking on where they were. You'd do that at night on a ship, using a tool called a sextant and measuring the position of the moon and stars. Reading the sky like a map. Celestial navigation. Those old guys came home and stuck to their habits. Took a moment out back to look up and get their bearings before turning in each night."

Gabe pauses, suddenly hearing how comforting he sounds. *Like a grown-up,* he thinks, a cross between Sal, who accepts the weird islander stuff, and his dad, who needs to explain it.

"Yeah." Paul nods. "We need some old-timer to take a reading on all this craziness and tell us what—"

Rrrrrr-wha-wha-rrrrr! A dog, large from the sound of his paws on dirt, scrambles to his feet in a nearby yard, growling and barking. The kids grab for each other and hurry along in wordless silence, some of the older ones holding younger hands.

At Sal's place, there are no lights in the windows.

Phee rushes over to greet her friends, saying, "You're here! Let's get going!"

Sal is already carrying boards on one shoulder, weaving rapidly in and out of the silvery darkness. "Get a move on, you blabber-lubbers," he calls softly.

Kids plus wood zip along beneath the stars and the moon until they reach the old navy base at the end of Tom Nevers Road. In what feels like the blink of an eye, all are standing in a cleared field, adding the backyard boards to an already huge pile.

No one feels tired or frightened. Maddie skips in circles, counting to ten over and over on her fingers.

Sal whistles. "I'll be. Whoever these ghosts are, they waste no time. This is quite a dream." His voice thrums with excitement. "Somehow, we're all moving in the same current and the ghosts know what we have in mind. The buildings *will* happen. I can feel it in my clickety-clank-fling-flong Folger soul!"

"Folger soldier!" Phee laughs, hugging her grandfather.

The better things feel, the wilder the language becomes, as if anything can be understood. But something else is happening: Sal has gone from saying little to saying lots. Gabe, too. It's as if the entire group feels oddly free.

Maddie is now flapping her arms like wings.

If Sal and the others were Maddie's age, they'd do it, too.

"How many people can say they've worked with ghosts?" All nod comfortably, thinking one of the others has said this.

But no one did, and it wasn't me.

CHAPTER 27

Pheeeee!

It's time for this Crier to shed a few tears.

If I concentrate, I can glimpse Sal as a boy, visiting my house after I was long gone. A whipped puppy of a kid with a thankless father, a man as nasty as a snapping turtle. Eliza offered refuge, with her starched curtains and ever-present wonders.

Now, oh, I can hardly bear to face it! Her neighbor Lydia Lyon's house is almost an empty shell. Even the curved lintel at the front door, that welcoming dip made by so many boots and soles—that smile of pine—has been tossed in the trash.

I have yet more distressing news.

Here it is: Eddy made a quiet call this morning from the hospital to the island company that owns the bulldozers and giant machines. He looked nervous. Sneaky. Like an adult doing something dishonest behind the backs of kids. I couldn't hear his words.

The doughnuts inside my door the other day, the ones that scared Eddy away—who set them out? It wasn't me. Or Eliza.

Many souls have lived in our house, I think to myself, realizing how little I know.

Will they step forward?

~

Herbie Pinkham is rarely at a loss, but lately he's been clueless. The crimes being carried out at "renovation" sites around town are accelerating, and he has no idea what to do.

The worst of it is that as an islander, he knows who's at least partly responsible. *Ghosts.* For real. He saw the fat-cat lawyer being jerked around by his own scarf, and there wasn't anybody doing it, if you follow me.

No one who wanted to be seen, at any rate.

When Gabe opens his eyes the next morning, he smells the Saturday happiness of waffles and maple syrup. And then he remembers. Yes! Last night's adventure with the lumber!

That massive pile, a harvest intended to help others who have no place to call home. Sal had explained it all to the Gang. This was unused, surplus land—the town of Nantucket had acquired it ages ago, and had barely thought of it in decades. And this beautiful, seasoned wood had been thrown away.

Now Gabe hears his dad yelling. "Whaaat? Someone's hauled wood out to the navy base and is building with it? What next!?"

Gabe is already out of bed and bounding down the stairs. "Really?" he asks his dad. "They're building?"

Herbie, despite his worries, glances sharply at the boy. "What do you know about this, Gabe? Huh? Because if you've heard the other kids talking, spit it out. I need you on my side here, no joke."

Gabe ducks his head over the butter plate, helping himself to a large pat. There is silence in the kitchen as both of his parents turn to look at him.

"Well, son?" His mom's voice is businesslike. "Dad's job is on the line, what with all these wrecked house sites and now this illegal construction, and no clue as to who is responsible. At least he can't seem to explain it or come up with any suspects. What it is that you know?"

Gabe pauses, a huge mouthful on his fork. "I know, well, that Sal Folger has had old boards piling up in his backyard at night. Lots of them."

"I know. That Sal, always has been a kinda lone wolf," the officer mutters. "Runs in his family. Never thought he'd break the law, though."

"Wait, Dad, no!" Gabe drops his fork. "He's not doing anything wrong!"

"And where exactly does Sal Folger say those boards are coming from?"

Gabe shrugs. "He doesn't know. Cross my heart. But he thinks it's the sites in town."

His dad reaches for his jacket. "Been to see him once. Well, gonna go back. Have a talk."

"Time out, Dad!" Gabe jumps up, sending his chair down with a crash. "Sal didn't do anything bad. He likes the idea of houses out on that unused land, houses for working people who can't afford them; he's talked about the housing problem for ages. Plus the idea of not wasting unwanted wood. You, Mom, and me have been on some of the Nantucket Hands picnics! It's no secret."

Herbie nods stiffly.

Gabe blurts, "And you *know* Sal's a generous guy. Please leave Sal out of it! He's shy—he'll be, he'll be—well, upset."

It was the wrong thing to say.

"I'M UPSET!" roared the officer. "My job is to keep the peace in this town, and at the moment a load of off-island people are angry because they think locals are ruining their properties. And now I hear that the boards that've been torn out of some historic houses—and I'm not saying that's right, this gutting business, don't get me wrong—are not only traveling around on their own but being used for an illegal project. Of course, I'm upset!"

"How about we go to Sal's together?"

Herbie pauses, surprised at his son's calm offer. The *we* is sweet. Gabe has never asked to go with him on a police matter before. He thinks for a moment, his mouth turned down like a disapproving flounder, his eyebrows up—as if being pulled in two directions.

"Get some clothes on," he tells his son. "We're off in five."

❧

Sal awoke that morning to the sound of a woman's voice sobbing, "Pheeeeeee! PHEE-EE-EEE!"

He sat up in bed, kicking off his quilts and scrambling into his trousers. This was a voice he knew.

Barefoot, he stood by the window listening. There was no wind to sigh, tease, or sing. No breeze draping a voice across a bad dream.

Heart thumping, Sal sank back down on his bed, thinking of his baby. Flossie, who had grown up without a mother and had loved to read and play and keep house with her father. Sal thought now of the blackberry jam she'd made every year, chatting through each part of the process—the picking, the crushing and boiling, the pouring into shining jars. She'd insisted on reading aloud to her father every night as soon as she knew how, doing what she always did: taking something he'd taught her and making it her own. She'd pulled away only as a young woman. When she met Phee's father, she had rushed off with her boyfriend to live on that houseboat and be independent.

And then came little Phee.

Even when Sal had begged his daughter to join him in the big house with her new family, she hadn't. Wouldn't. Then came that stormy night, when they'd left Phee on the boat and the Coast Guard had found her, no thanks to her parents.

Flossie had been furious with Sal when he became Phee's guardian, but was it his fault? He'd stepped in only to help save them all.

After Phee's rescue, Flossie had rushed off. Although Phee had never seemed particularly worried about when her mother was returning, Sal reassured her that when Flossie was back, the three of them would live together in the Folger home.

Come to think of it, Phee had been reaching out to her mom since Nantucket Hands started. Sal smiled in the dark. Had Nantucket Hands made Phee want her mom to come home and join the fight?

Now Sal rubs his eyes with his knuckles. *Sobbing, Flossie sobbing for her little girl . . .* He tiptoes into Phee's room, just to check. His granddaughter's dark hair ripples across the pillow like eelgrass at low tide. She sighs peacefully in her sleep.

His Phee. His Floss. Sal can't get rid of a flicker of fear. Has something gone wrong? His forehead creases into lines that echo the ridges on a sandbar. Nah! His grown-up girl is fine, Sal tells himself, heading downstairs and plunking logs into the woodstove to start the fire.

She's probably on her way home.

Dreams can be gut twisters.

Sal is snoozing in one of the rockers when Officer Pinkham's feet clump up the kitchen stairs. Gabe's face peers in the side window. Sal knows kids' expressions, and Gabe—well, Gabe is warning him.

Herbie rap-raps on the window.

"Why, hello, you two. Do come in." Sal holds open the door.

Gabe swallows, a horribly loud gulp followed by a log

fizz-huffing in the stove. Perhaps the wood is trying to cover for him.

"Some breakfast?" Sal asks.

The officer looks around the room and his face softens. "No, no, thanks . . . boy, it feels good in here on a cold morning. Like old times. The house *smells* right, you know? Some of these new places, you might be inside a department store on the mainland. They stink of plastic and room fresheners. I mean, no heart at all—" Herbie Pinkham stops, realizing he's babbling inappropriately.

Gabe steps comfortably in front of his dad and Herbie frowns. "Yeah, I like this kitchen," Gabe adds quietly. "Me and Phee and some of the other Nantucket Hands kids, we meet here after school sometimes. While you and Mom are still at work, Dad."

"Hrrrumpa-dun." Herbie clears his throat, too. "Yes, thanks, Sal. Kind of you."

"Not at all, I thoroughly enjoy their company," Sal says formally.

Gabe realizes right then that his dad feels he has to be official in front of his son, at least with all these ghostly goings-on, and that Sal understands that.

"Speaking of *company*," Herbie trumpets, "I see the pile out behind is gone now, and understand a whole bunch of old wood from construction site dumpsters turned up last night on town property in the Southeast Quarter. Out Tom Nevers way. Looks like someone's started to build with it. Know anything about that, Sal?"

Just as the older man clears his throat to respond, a small empty rocker by the fireplace goes back and forth on its own. Ever so gently, as if the person sitting in it is thinking. This gives Gabe a chance to sneak a *didn't-tell-him-about-last-night* look to Sal. The old man then turns to the officer, whose eyes are on the chair.

Sal steps over and puts a foot on one of the rocker's rungs. It stops.

"Old house, you know" is all he had to say.

"Yes, well, yup, yes sirree," Herbie mutters, his eyes big. "But about that business—"

Thump-thump, clunk-bonk-clunk! Familiar feet on the stairs. "Good morning, everyone!" Phee sings out, as if not at all surprised to see Herbie and Gabe.

Good, Gabe thinks to himself. *She's been listening.*

"How about you take us all out to the old navy base, Dad?" Gabe asks quickly. "To see this building stuff you're talking about. Sounds interesting!" He hopes Sal and Phee get the message.

Hands on his hips, the officer glances nervously at the rocker. "Okay," he says slowly. "Don't see why not. Maybe you'll also have some ideas about what's been going on lately at the 'renovation' sites in town, Sal. Maybe you can help me out."

"Happy to, I'm sure," Sal says.

As soon as the door closes behind the four of them, the rocker starts moving again, a little faster this time.

Creeeak-crack-creakity-sneak!

CHAPTER 28

The thrill of a voice

When the group arrives at the navy base, the kids gasp. Sal turns quickly toward them and says, "Well, someone sure is working hard to make our Nantucket Hands dream come true! What say, kids? Look!"

As if they hadn't just been there the night before.

But truly, there *is* something astounding going on. Since Sal and the kids left last night, someone else brought a load of cinder blocks for foundations. And under a huge tarp sits a bevy of household appliances. A new dishwasher! Three clothes washers, an electric stove, and two brand-new-looking refrigerators! A flock of microwave units.

I smile, thinking of all the housework this saves.

"Yow!" Herbie says, walking gingerly around the lumber, building supplies, and appliances. "Looks like someone took a haul from the dump; crazy how much good stuff gets pulled out of houses when they change hands. Seen it happen myself, many a time. Well, I'll be."

"Nice." Sal nods. "Not to see all that wasted, don't you think, Herbie? Like old times on the island. When everyone used every little bit of string, so to speak. That, and helped each other do it."

As if he's forgotten for a moment why they're there, the officer nods happily. "Yeah, that's the way," he says to the two kids. "The way both Sal and I were brought up here, to share." Not wanting to burst the bubble of good feeling, Gabe and Phee smile innocently, looking around at the area as if for the first time.

Gabe, feeling a rush of warmth for his dad, gives him a quick thumbs-up. To his surprise, his dad winks in return, as if the two of them share a secret.

Gabe wonders if his dad knows more than he's letting on. If so, he isn't as much of a stiff toothpick as Gabe had thought.

"But, Sal," Herbie says, strolling away from the kids as if the older man should come with him. Sal does.

"Say," he continues, glancing back to be sure they are out of hearing range. "Didn't want to ask you about this with the kids listening, but let's cut to the chase. You've heard about all the craziness going on at the so-called renovation sites, the accidents and the broken stuff, the splashed paint, the flooding. Well, ah, I'm wondering if some of that could be *ghosts*."

"Ahh," Sal says, a twinkle in his eye. "Angry ghosts. Don't see why not, do you?"

"Between the two of us, no," the officer says. "But officially, how can I say that to off-island owners and their dad-blasted lawyers and such? I mean, I'm in a tight spot."

"You are," Sal agreed. "A tight spot."

As the two men walk and talk, arms grown-up-style behind their backs, Gabe and Phee wander slowly around the area with the old boards.

"Hey, Gabe!"

"What?"

"Look at these big footprints! Those weren't made by any one of us! They're fresh, you know? The group who came later last night worked *hard*. Think they know about us?"

Gabe shrugs. "Got to. All the wood we brought! Maybe they think we're as mysterious as they are."

The two friends stare at each other, not exactly sure what Gabe means but sensing it's true.

"I'm wondering about the kids I saw when I was being the lure, on my own. Whether *they* know about this." Gabe looks serious.

Phee is quiet for a moment. "You mean, whether they're okay. Still around. Or whether they're gone."

"Yeah, it's all been quieter with Eddy in the hospital, but . . ." Gabe breaks off. "I wonder how long a ghost can stay strong? I can't help wondering about the boy with the hat in Lydia Lyon's home, working so hard to get my attention, and his little sister with the doll. And then those three kids in the Pine Street house, dashing around like mad."

"I know." Phee frowns. "Eddy Nold may feel better soon and do something even bigger and nastier."

Ooohhh, Mary here! I wish I were a flesh-and-blood Crier and everyone stopped to listen! They're right, Eddy's up to no good, it's already happening . . . I ring my bell wildly, my heart sick with what I cannot share.

When Herbie and Sal stroll over, they find the friends sitting quietly on a stack of lumber.

Herbie is reassured by how subdued they look. "Ready, kids?" he asks cheerfully.

He means *ready to go* . . . but I raise my horn and call out, "Yes, YES! Get ready! Ready to save us alllllll!"

Herbie glances around, startled. "Anyone hear that?" he asks the group. When Sal, Phee, and Gabe look blankly at him, he shrugs and mutters, "Cop ears. Sounded like a woman shouting, but gotta be some kinda birdcall."

I am thrilled. It's me, me, ME! Mary W. Chase!

This is the first time since I became a ghost that anyone living has heard me.

Hope flips the pages in my heart.

I think now of my cozy home, with its blue teapot and twinkly copper pots, and then of the destruction in all those other homes and the children trying so hard to get someone's attention. Some who waved, others who pinched . . . and then the flesh-and-blood Old North Gang, filled with big plans and perhaps in danger of falling into the hands of some of the more dangerous spirits on this island, the ones who've been causing accidents and injuries.

The ones whose lives were ruthless and hard, and who may not hesitate to *use* these kids to stop someone like Eddy Nold.

The ones who will defend their homes at any cost, and who can blame them?

Criers watch and tell, but I'll do more than that. A surge of determination and rage fills my heart.

If needed, I will scream. I'll scream loud enough to wake an army of the living and the dead.

Phee goes to bed that night longing for her mother. Flossie of the jingly bracelets, sparkly stars, and hugs. Flossie Folger, who had been a little girl in this same house with Sal.

Phee feels guilty. She has a sinking feeling that she hasn't been good about staying in touch with her mom, not really, and doesn't think about her enough.

She *does* miss her, and hopes her mom somehow knows.

She'll talk to Sal in the morning. That always makes everything better.

But then the day whirls forward and she doesn't do it, maybe because Sal has enough on his plate these days. After breakfast, she and Sal head to the dump to check on the latest, cool air nipping at their noses. Neither has to explain their curiosity to the other.

Once out there, Sal circles the area reserved for metals, electronics, and such. He plans to ask a few questions.

The man on duty, however, can't seem to make time for him. Perhaps he just doesn't want to. Sal understands. The guy has earphones and is speaking intently in another language as he waves the trucks through to unload their goods.

Sal, never one to press, simply watches. One shiny appliance follows another. "Boggles the mind," he mutters to himself. So much waste. The thought of someone with a big heart and a large truck somehow sneaking a whole mess of these goods out of the dump at night and getting them to the navy base, though! Now, *that* was a warming thought.

As Sal pulls his sock hat down over his ears and rubs his hands together, he calculates how many houses could be supplied with what he's seeing.

Phee watches the flow at the Take It or Leave It shed with much the same delight. Crows and seagulls swoop and dive around the visitors.

Watching the crows hunt for color and sparkle, Phee has an odd idea. Suddenly she imagines how much they would love her mother's crescent of stars, the one she always wore in her hair.

Phee shakes the thought away, reminding herself that when her mom returns home, she'll have that crescent of stars in her hair, as she always did.

And speaking of home, there are so many almost-new tables! Chairs with maybe one broken rung! Curtains and rugs with a stain or two! And oh, look! A whole crate of mismatched candlesticks and kerosene lamps! Enough to make any house built from old boards more than comfortable.

Phee can't wait to tell the Coffin kids and the Ramos twins about what's arrived in Tom Nevers since the group left last night. That is, if Gabe hasn't done it already.

Exactly how, she wonders, could the Gang get together with the ghosts who are doing so much work? And then she pictures the flash of people she saw when running down the street with Gabe, on that day when the church bells all rang like mad.

That warm-feeling arm! And the red sleeve . . . The face that looked so much like her mom's. Had she imagined it?

Sal called that kind of thing a *confluence*: when two streams flow together. Ghosts flowing into living hands, the two working together, or was it hands flowing into living ghosts?

Phee doesn't really know what she's wondering, but the back-and-forth of it feels good in her head. When Sal pedals over, an odd shadow flits across his creased, stubbly cheeks, but he says only, "Phoebe Folger Antoine, let's get ourselves home. It's time."

On the way back to town, Phee is filled with light. It's a no-reason happiness, maybe simply because she and Sal were helping others. Flying along on a mission, carrying a sparkly secret, weightless as dump crows in the bright November chill.

That must be it.

CHAPTER 29

An unwanted swim

The next morning, a man almost dies beneath the Pine Street home, where the basement has been excavated.

A senior member of Eddy's crew got a phone call from the hospital the night before. His boss asked him to check on the abandoned sites, but early, before the rest of the town awoke. This worker understood that Eddy wanted him to get a good look at the problem areas but not be seen doing it.

"Less said, the better," Eddy explained to him. Sitting up in his hospital bed that morning, the contractor waited to hear back from his employee. Eddy owes his workers money, and the house owners owe *him* money. A job is a job, and Eddy is nothing if not responsible in that way.

An hour later, his worker is in the emergency room.

I'm there as well, unseen. I listen.

Eddy, horrified at the news, limps in to see this man. The two talk.

"I was standing at the edge of the dig, ya know?" the worker whispers. Deep under electric blankets, he's as colorless as a fish egg. "Saw some runoff water in the foundation area, as no one's pumped the last day or so. Suddenly the hydrant nearby goes on *full blast*, no one near it, and water pours into the hole. I rush to turn the thing off. No go. I grab my phone to call the fire department for help and my phone just, well, flips out of my hand. *Whissh!* It flies through the air as if someone *threw* it. Falls in the water, which is starting to look like the nastiest swimming pool you've ever seen.

"I step closer to the edge, hardly believing what just happened and how fast the hole is filling. I turn away to go for help when I'm *pushed*. Got the shock of my life. Like someone gave me a shove.

"Suddenly I'm tumbling head over heels, eating mud and rolling toward that freezing-cold mess. Couldn't seem to get a grip on a root or pipe to stop myself. *Splash*, I'm under! And here's where things get really nuts. I bobbed to the surface but couldn't get back up. Just *wasn't able* to get on my feet. Like someone kept knocking my legs out from under me. Must've been a sight, big old me thrashing around and shouting down there in shallow water. No one came. I finally gave up and floated on my back, thinking, 'What a way to go,' knowing it might be hours before someone found my body.

"Each time my face started to sink below the surface, I kind of jolted myself awake. I thought of my wife and kids. I prayed.

"My arms and legs got numb pretty fast. Things stopped hurting. It was then I saw a middle-aged woman peering over the side of the foundation. She looked kinda old-timer-y, had a long skirt and all, hair back in a bun, and she was carrying a bell and a horn. Weird, huh?"

Eddy nods, but not as though he's really listening.

I knew it! Now I've been heard AND seen! What next?

I grin with delight! I could dance around the hospital room! *Silly men! Watch out! I'm right next to you!*

The worker pauses and looks around, as if he'd heard my thoughts.

"Go on," Eddy prompts him.

The man does. "'Hey!' I called, shakin' like all get-out. 'Please help me! I'm goin' down here!'

"This next part is crazy. I then felt something or someone pulling me, but not with adult hands, more like lots of little ones, helping me slowly up the bank. Musta been dozens, because my wet clothing weighed a ton and I don't remember climbing. Guess it was just mind over matter, you know?

"The ambulance found me passed out in my truck."

Huh, I think to myself. *Let me tell you what really happened.*

When that man looked up at me, right into my eyes, his face brightened with hope and I spun around toward the empty house, filled with energy. I didn't know if I'd imagined being visible, but I rang my bell and blew on the horn like mad. "Hey, kids! You three in here! Call your friends! Help this fellow—he hasn't done anything wrong and he shouldn't die. He's a *worker*! NOW!"

Seconds later, the man found himself standing.

I didn't see anyone helping him and he no longer seemed to see me. But, even though I'd disappeared in his eyes, we both knew the truth.

Once he got back in his truck, he wept. "Thank you, thank you," he muttered. I wanted to weep, too, knowing he'd die despite my help if he couldn't warm up. I tried to rub his back, but my hands went right through his body. He was too cold to drive and soon passed out. The ghost kids seemed to be gone, but a neighbor walking a dog came around the corner and found the man slumped, his clothing coated with ice, in his truck.

An ambulance raced him to the hospital.

"Hypothermia," the admitting nurse told him, patting his hand. "You were almost a goner. Lucky someone walked by."

Not only that, I think proudly to myself.

Have I crossed some kind of dividing line? I was *heard* by Herbie, then *seen* by someone who needed me, and then *worked with* a bunch of young ghosts to help save this man's life! An innocent man under attack was *rescued*! What next?

How much stronger can I get?

Does this mean we ghosts are gaining power?

I pause for a moment in the corner of the emergency room, chilled by the questions that remain.

Who turned on the water hydrant and who pushed this man, almost to his death?

Who else is back?

~

"Can I help it?" roars Officer Pinkham when he hears the news about Eddy's worker. Veins stand out on his neck.

"Who can control a bunch of ghosts?" he shouts, thunking his coffee mug on the kitchen counter. "This is Nantucket, holy mag*nees*us! You know the stories as well as I do! And you know I can't speak freely." He grabs his forehead with both hands, as if to keep his head from exploding.

Gabe's mom had suggested that he ask for extra police protection at the sites.

The boy glances at the picture of his great-grandma Hepsa and wonders if *she* could control what's going on. Maybe she'll jump in and help him, his dad, and the others, seen and unseen. Gabe thinks about suggesting it, but then realizes his parents might get suspicious if he does.

Right then, the picture of Gabe's great-grandparents swings gently from side to side, making a quiet scraping sound against the wall. The three Pinkhams freeze. Gabe smiles and Herbie gulps. Gabe's mom sees her son's expression and frowns.

Meanwhile in the hospital, the worker dozes after his chat with the boss. Eddy is back in his room. He looks angry.

"Unfair," he mutters to himself. "Outrageous. If the cops can't stop this nonsense, then I will!"

CHAPTER 30

A harpoon escapes

Sal and Phee stand before a blackened frying pan that sizzles on the stove. A delicious smell fills the kitchen as the police officer bursts in the door.

"Why, hello, Herbie," Sal says pleasantly. "Nice to see so much of you."

The younger man blurts, "I need you, Sal. Need you bad. You're the only one who might figure out something to do here. The old homes in town, I mean, maybe it's not the houses, but something *in* the houses . . ."

Sal squints at Phee. "Okay by you?" he asks.

"Go!" Phee waves him off.

The door closes behind them. On its own.

Phee hardly notices. Their Folger home has always done things its own way.

A change of heart is hard to admit, but Herbie Pinkham is changing. First, he can't seem to stop talking. "You understand the island, Sal. A lot of these newcomers just don't. And here's how I see it: When it was just the matter of a new appliance or two, plumbing and electric, the spirits of the island weren't disturbed. They never minded us replacing rotted wood or adding something to cook on or take a bath in. But lately, this business of buying an old house and then trashing the inside of it—well, I overheard one old-timer stop and ask a contractor if he'd ever thought about what he was doing.

"'Destroying a treasure, that's what you're doing!' the islander said. 'It's wrong, I tell you—like buying a lovely old desk or table for a lot of money, and then instead of using and enjoying it, making the wood glow, you chip-chop it up for firewood. Insanity, that's what's going on around here!' I had to smile."

"Ignorance of our island ways," Sal agrees quietly. "That and a lack of feeling for Nantucket's homemade self. Maybe those owners never stopped to think about the one-of-a-kind nature of the house they'd bought. Or to defend it against an off-island engineer who said, 'Nah, rip it all out! It's junk!' Maybe they never stopped to wonder whether our old wood could actually be valuable as is."

Sal scratches his head through his sock hat. "Let's say this lumber is steeped in layers of living, meaning people's lives. As if we humans are like tea leaves soaking in water, and the teapot is the house. All these old buildings have flavors and stains because of what's gone on inside them. And maybe the island has finally reached a level beyond which this rip-and-toss behavior can't be tolerated. Not for any kind of money. The balance is off."

The officer looks momentarily confused. "Tea," he repeats. "Balance. You mean we've reached—what's that thing people say? A spilling point?"

"A tipping point," Sal says. "A point at which things can't go on. Not without a whole blim-blam of trouble."

"And by helping to do something good with all that wasted stuff, and including our kids, you were trying to make things better."

"You got it," Sal says. "So you know about our *lunar* last night?"

"Yeah." Herbie thumps a fist into the palm of his other hand and sighs. "I mean, that kind of jaunt is against everyone's family rules, but I put two and two together and then didn't know what to do with four, if you follow my drift. I just didn't know how to admit it to the kids. Or you! I'm glad you did that with them. Guess I've been a fool for law and order at a time when our whole way of life is under attack.

"What'm I gonna do, Sal? What on earth am I gonna do? There's no way I can stop this, and—"

"—you don't really want to," Sal finishes for the younger man.

"*Don't really want to,*" the police officer repeats slowly. "It's all over, Sal," he mutters. "I'm cooked. Done."

The two men pause at one of the "renovation" sites that had been abandoned a few days before. The front door is boarded up, and half the old shingles are gone. The kitchen wall has been removed and a tarpaulin covers what remains of the old corner posts. It hangs bone-still—a sad, blue flag.

Suddenly, the edge of this plastic sheet lifts on its own. Up, up, up. Soon a lovely old beam lying outside, a massive piece of lumber from some long-ago tree, floats from the ground, wobbles in place as if trying to decide which way to go, and slips inside beneath the tarp. With no workers visible, the plastic drops back and all is still again.

Herbie snorts, a sound that isn't a laugh. It's more a sob. Sal gives his shoulder a squeeze.

Officer Pinkham heads home, ready to tell his wife and Gabe that he's going to resign.

Shuffling in the front door, he hears *Brrrt! Brrrt!* A call is coming over the kitchen transmitter from the station.

A note on the table tells him that Becky is doing errands and Gabe is with the Gang, at Sal's.

He listens to the call.

"Whaaaaat?" he shouts, fury turning his face red. Slamming back out the door, Herbie rushes downtown.

Nantucket has had a Whaling Museum housed in an old candle factory for many years. It's packed with handmade items: scrimshaw, baskets, chairs, silver, every kind of whaling equipment, souvenirs brought home by the whalemen, portraits, and seascapes galore. In November the museum closes early, and it had been locked for the better part of an hour. As Herbie Pinkham arrives, he sees the front door of this venerable institution swing wide open on its own and then bang closed. A small group of neighbors stand out in front.

"Just watchin' things," one woman reports. "Makin' sure nothin' gets out. Door has done this at least three times."

"The noises in there—not made by a person," her husband adds. "Just warning ya, Herbie, might want to get backup. Sounds like that there whale skeleton is swimming around inside."

Gabe! The officer needs him. "Bad," he mutters aloud.

He asks one of the islanders watching to find Gabe and tell him to get downtown as fast as possible, bringing the rest of the Gang. Sal, too.

After all, Herbie reasons to himself, those kids and Sal Folger won't waste any time doubting, and the ghosts—if that's what they are—will recognize them as *helpers* on the right side of things. Hadn't they all been in on moving a bunch of rescued wood the night before?

Ten minutes later, the kids trot down the street, minus Maddie, who's home with Grandma Sue. Gabe, Phee, Maria and Markus Ramos, Cyrus and Paul Coffin. Phee explains that Sal is out revisiting the "renovation" sites in town, having had a sudden idea about "the crazy stuff" happening there.

"His idea was simple," she says. "Shouldn't we be talking to *them* and not just each other?" Phee glances around at the group.

Them. Herbie grunts. He hopes Sal knows what he's doing.

The kids by his side, the police officer walks softly to the Whaling Museum door and listens. *Whang!* The door flies open and bonks him on the forehead. A harpoon, an old one, bobs into view, dances sideways, and falls to the sidewalk.

Hear me, all doubters!

Paul reaches down and picks up the weapon. Slowly. Carefully. "Okay to bring this back in?" he asks in a loud voice, pointing the sharp tip, scarred and twisted in some long-ago battle with a whale, away from everyone. "Seems like it might get mislaid out here."

"Super-valuable tool," Markus adds, looking at no one in particular. "Whoever used it won't like seeing it outside this building. Might think it was being tossed away. Thrown to the fishes."

At that, the harpoon yanks out of Paul's hand and bounces back toward the front door.

Yes, as if someone is carrying it.

The group trots after. All six kids slip easily through the opening and vanish inside, the locals sighing and tut-tutting, shifting from one sneaker to the other. As Herbie steps firmly after the kids, something stamps on his boot. Hard.

"Oww!" the officer shouts. Pulling his foot back but tightening his grip on the door, he asks in a calmer tone, "May I enter? I'm here to make peace. Really."

Fwishhh! His police hat is knocked off his head and sails neatly into a nearby hydrangea bush. When Herbie doesn't react, not even to smooth down his ruffled hair, the door swings slightly toward him and he mutters, "Thanks, you won't regret it." He steps inside bareheaded.

I, Mary Chase, am in my element. *Listen, all you who buy and sell! Know first how little you may know! The Crier is no liar!*

I don't pretend to understand all that I report, but as the Crier I'll continue to make noise until silenced.

Oh me oh my, even as I speak, I now can't seem to control this bell and horn. They jump in my hand.

I press both against my skirts and slip silently inside.

CHAPTER 31

Floating and falling

Heavy objects are flying. When Herbie catches up to the kids, he stands, mouth open, watching.

It is one thing to accept that Nantucket probably has ghosts and see unexplained footprints at the shoreline—or to believe that hauntings really do happen at "renovation" sites, and that they can either help or hurt the living. Or that things move around at night while the island sleeps, a happening Sal seems to think is almost normal. But this! Here they are, real-live spirits, invisible but clearly hard at work.

Well, I'll be, I can hear Herbie Pinkham thinking to himself. *Never imagined I'd actually witness such a sight! A game changer, that's what this is.*

I see Gabe sneaking a look at his father, who returns it in kind. That unguarded exchange is the beginning of an understanding that catches in both of their throats. Gabe looks away as if it's no big deal, but it is.

First, there is the nineteenth-century whaleboat. Equipped with six long oars, this small vessel was used by the men who chased and harpooned the whales. Normally sitting on a platform beneath the skeleton, it is now up in the air and traveling toward the second floor, as if being carried sideways up the stairs. Occasionally, one side of the boat or another bumps a railing and the thing pauses, steadying itself. The oars drift along in its wake, and three or four of the most beautiful harpoons fly slowly upward at a gentle, forty-five-degree angle.

Herbie and the kids freeze, hardly breathing, until the objects thumpity-bump along the second-floor hall and disappear from sight. The group follows this invisible current. The policeman finds himself cautioning them to keep a steady hand on the stair rail—they should hold tight if airborne. Sounds crazy, but who knows? He raises a finger to his lips as they climb, although the kids are already dead silent.

The officer hopes that if they can't see the ghosts, perhaps the ghosts can't see them, either. Now Herbie has an all-too-vivid flash of the lawyer he'd seen strangled by his own scarf, and right out in the open. No need to get these ghosts mad.

Or madder than they already are.

Even in the gloom of the unlit museum, the group of one adult and six kids can see that the air is filled with objects. As the whaleboat floats into the special-exhibits room at the end of the hall, a flow of treasures follows.

Scrimshaw bobs by. A whalebone pie crimper with a mermaid on the handle dances next to Phee like a strange butterfly; yellowed whale teeth covered with scenes of ships and curvy ladies drift past, one following another. Two canes with an ivory hand at the top bounce along, as if being carried. An old marketing basket and several lightship baskets come next, one almost hitting Maria on the head. She ducks and giggles.

The basket pauses.

The kids and Herbie, who've been gliding silently along the edges of the corridor, freeze midstep. A moment or two later, the basket travels on.

Now comes a spindle-back chair, some braided rugs, a stack of old patchwork quilts, and a few floorboards that look as if they might have been borrowed from the navy base pile, one an astounding three feet wide. Next, an assortment of wooden and iron latches, and a rocking horse minus most of its paint. All are things that could easily have come from Sal and Phee's home. In fact,

Phee thinks, the rocking horse looks *a lot* like the one from their attic.

Herbie and the kids crowd around the door to the exhibition room, their faces awash in wonder. Objects are alive: A tea tray or jug or candlestick floats to a certain spot, and then abruptly changes direction. An embroidered pillow and a flock of pewter spoons sink gently to the floor and then take off again, as if the ghosts are trying to decide where to put them or as if these things have invisible wings.

Phee, as Sal's granddaughter, notices immediately that every item was no doubt made by an islander, and by hand. *Our Nantucket hands*—Phee smiles to herself, hearing Sal's words in her head. She can't wait to tell him about all of this.

Just when things can't get much stranger, they do: The longer the group stands motionless in the doorway, the more clearly they hear the faintest smattering of voices. As if someone is slowly, slowly turning up the volume on a radio.

"Here . . ." is followed by "Really?" and then, "Yes, yes!" The level stops rising just before the sentences become clear. All kids have overheard adults through closed doors. This is exactly the sound: language filtered by wood. Something going on, something the listener isn't a part of.

Gabe thinks of what he heard in Lydia Lyon's house on the day he saw those bubbles of everyday living. I think of what I used to hear in my very own home, at the lonely times.

Herbie strains to hear but can't catch as much as the kids, perhaps because he has older ears.

Gabe squints hard at a photograph propped against a far wall, one of a dog looking out to sea. The dog has his head back, howling in profile. He's alone on the beach, big surf breaking in front of him.

"It's Ghost!" Gabe whispers excitedly. "It can't be, but it looks *exactly* like Ghost! Haven't seen him in ages, but I *know* that's him!"

Forgetting where he is, Gabe steps quickly into the room and calls out, "Look!"

Phee rushes to his side, grabs his arm, and hisses, "Shhhh!"

Invisible feet thump closer and something collides hard with Phee, sending her crashing to the floor.

CHAPTER 32

Out, quick!

Herbie is at Phee's side in a flash. She gasps, the wind partly knocked out of her. Gabe's dad scoops her up.

"Hurry, kids! *Out!*" he orders in a whisper, suddenly terrified that the entire group, children he's allowed to linger in the museum with him, might be under attack.

What had he, a trained police officer, been thinking? These ghosts have some serious weapons, including harpoons and oars!

The kids and officer hurry down the hall, wishing at that moment that they were already safely outside. A chair floats to the doorway behind them and then clatters down as if dropped. The group rushes on, Phee breathing more normally but still whisked along in Herbie's arms.

The sidewalk outside the museum is now empty.

Coughing but embarrassed, Phee struggles to get down. Herbie lowers her gently to a bench and steps back.

"Should never have called you kids," he mutters under his breath.

"We're glad you did, Dad," Gabe pipes up. "And what just happened was my fault, not yours."

"Mmph," Herbie grunts, but blinks rapidly, looking thankful.

Phee, oddly, seems the least disturbed of everyone. "I smelled lemons," she croaks, her voice filled with wonder. "Like my mom was around when I got knocked down. And I've gotta check on Sal," she adds.

The rest of the Gang freezes when Phee mentions Flossie. Could her mom be *a ghost*? And if so, isn't Phee upset?

Herbie, trained to help those who've had a shock, decides to focus on her concerns about Sal.

"I'll revisit the sites your grandfather and I were at earlier," he tells Phee in his official voice, then studies the group, who suddenly look small and vulnerable.

The idea of chasing wandering kids as well as a missing grandfather is too much. *Too dang much,* Herbie thinks irritably to himself. *Bad idea. Like trying to catch baitfish with your bare hands. Drat this job. Hate it! Someone else can take a turn getting blamed for every goldarn thing that goes wrong around here.*

He wonders if the island has passed the point at which its ghosts can be reasoned with. Perhaps, as with Phee in the Whaling Museum just now, something will go after Sal or the kids at any time, given an opportunity. Lord knows there are many excavations to fall into. Razor-sharp table saws and cutting blades.

If anything were to happen to Gabe . . .

"How about you guys all head over to the Folger place and wait for me there? You, too, son," the officer barks as he leaves.

Giving an order makes him feel better. As an adult whose job is to be responsible for everyone's safety, though, he knows that he is no match for whatever is making trouble.

Soon he finds himself stopping in front of one of the abandoned "renovation" sites. He moves orange hazard cones from the middle of the street and then freezes, mouth open in horror.

There, sticking out of a basement window, is one of Sal's legs.

CHAPTER 33

Boards that bite

"Sal! What on earth! You okay?" The officer flops down on all fours in the mud. The growl of a machine pulses from inside the building. He reaches out gingerly to touch bare skin on the protruding leg.

It vanishes inside and both men shout with horror at the same moment. As the officer rocks back on his heels, rubbing dirt across his mouth, Sal's sock hat bobs into view.

The older man is the first to speak. "Thought you were a vengeful ghost!" he blurts, his face the color of a beet.

"Thought you were a corpse!" Herbie shoots back. "*What* are you doing in there?"

"This is one of the houses with the worst damage—you know, tools thrown around, paint splashed, things like that." Sal pauses to glance over his shoulder. "One of the ones the off-island professionals came to see. I was *talking* to it, I mean *them*. Asking how I could help. Suddenly the heating unit over there clicked on. I was concerned about fire, so I decided I'd better slip in through this window and turn the thing off, but then my sneaker got wedged in between boards. No, let's be honest: It was more like the boards jumped up and grabbed my leg."

Shaking his head, the older man bends over to feel his knee. "Yep, still in one piece. Guess it's good you came and scared the dickens out of the situation, because I might've been stuck so long that I passed out and turned into a piece of bacon with that heater cranking. Hot as Hades."

Herbie looks down, realizing he's been sinking. "Scared the dang-blasted chowder out of me, too, no kidding," he mutters, struggling to get up. "Thought someone was planning to use your leg for a paint stirrer."

Sal now struggles to turn off the heater, but can't. The ON switch won't move.

"Leave it," the officer calls in. "I'll find whoever's in charge. Let's get you out of there."

After a messy scramble, both men rest quietly on the curb. Mud is smeared across their clothing. "Glad I put on a clean uniform this morning," Herbie says.

"Yeah. Glad I put on my best pants for visiting," Sal says, looking at a shredded knee. "And newest dump shirt," he adds, examining a rip in his latest Take It or Leave It find.

The men glance at each other and grin.

"Know what?" the officer asks.

"That's what!" Sal's quick smile turns wistful. "Seems like yesterday that you and Flossie and I played that game, when the two of you were schoolkids."

"But that's *it*." The officer nods. "That *is* what! They want to be left alone to do things their own way. Clear as day."

"But," Sal says slowly, "you're a policeman. You can't allow this."

The younger man throws up his hands. "Why not?" he says. "Had it with being blamed for all this dangerous tomfoolery. Followed the kids into the empty Whaling Museum just now and, oh boy, Sal—you shoulda been there. Stuff flying around. Phee got knocked down somethin' bad but she seems fine—"

Sal stares at him. "And you didn't tell me right away?"

"Well . . ." All is quiet for a beat. "I know you're more matter-of-fact about ghosts than I am, so I was trying to see it in a calm light. And she mentioned something about smelling lemons, like her mom was there with her when it happened. We were all kinda rattled by that, but she didn't seem upset. And now I'm wondering, what if the ghosts that've been acting up are somehow *luring* the kids closer so that they can turn on them?"

"You think we're headed for a nasty climax, the way a school of sharks can behave once blood gets in the water," Sal says slowly. "You sent the kids back to my place. Told them to stay there. Alone."

Not a word is spoken as both men hurry toward the Folger house, Sal limping.

Once the two are out of sight, the heating unit in the basement switches off, the coils clicking as they cool in the darkening room.

~

When the kids get to the Folger house, they step into the kitchen and freeze. Something upstairs is thumping and dragging furniture.

Ba-bonk! SCREE-thunk!

Phee whispers, "Sounds like it's coming from my mom's old room. That's not Sal. No one ever stays there and—well, it might or might not be her."

She tiptoes toward the bottom of the stairs.

"Phee! Stop! You nuts?" Gabe hisses. "You just got attacked in the museum, and it *hurt*. Come on, we'll go together, but let's each grab a piece of wood or something. You know, so we can defend ourselves."

"Against *ghosts*?" Cyrus asks, knowing it isn't a real question.

"Come on." Paul elbows him. "Feels better not to be empty-handed."

Armed with kindling, the Gang creeps slowly up the stairwell, Phee leading the way so they can avoid squeaky treads. The noises continue. *Whack!* Something like a heavy book falls to the floor.

The door to Flossie's old room is ajar. Sal and Phee always leave it closed.

As she slowly pushes it open, Phee distinctly hears a swift intake of breath from inside. Next, the murmur of a female voice—or is it the swish of water against their old houseboat?—and a whispered "*Phee?* Is that you?"

CHAPTER 34

A rumpled bed

Eyes huge, Phee peers around the corner.

The room is empty.

The bed, however, is rumpled as though someone has slept in it, and the pillow is dented. The dresser that Sal had pushed in front of Flossie's empty closet years ago—for some reason, Phee had been afraid of that closet—has been moved. A heavy picture book from a dusty bookcase, a volume Phee recognizes from Sal's childhood, is on the floor. *Grimm's Fairy Tales.*

Phee shudders. She's always hated that book. It's filled with kids getting tortured, lost, or killed. Nasty stuff from the old days.

The others behind her try to peer in as well, but Phee backs up, closing the door gently.

"No one inside," she says. "Just house ghosts moving stuff around. Not hurting anything."

She doesn't mention the bed or the dresser. No one else says they heard a voice, nor do they ask what a house ghost is.

The messed-up quilt makes Phee's heart pound. It's almost as if her mom had returned secretly, to help out.

But if so, where *is* she?

Could this mean she's *died*? The word glints, sharp and dangerous, and the hallway swims with sudden tears. Phee blinks them back.

Died! Died, died, DIED!

Slamming her mind shut on the word, Phee feels sure this isn't the case. Flossie always *makes things happen*, doesn't she? She wouldn't die.

Phee is not in the habit of talking about Flossie, at least not with other kids, and truthfully—well, she isn't quite sure what she feels about her mom.

There is love, always, but also a fear of being hurt. Of disappointment. After all, what if Flossie never comes home from off-island? Isn't it better not to miss her too much? Phee knows she and Sal have a great life together. A life other kids envy, one that includes everyday evenings by the fire and using all that the island offers—making fish-bone jewelry, wild grapevine wreaths, and bayberry candles. Scavenging at the dump and cooking up a mission like Nantucket Hands.

While tiptoeing back downstairs with her friends, Phee hears the old latch on Flossie's bedroom door click open again, ever so softly.

Someone is listening, Phee thinks to herself.

She doesn't tell the others.

CHAPTER 35

The clang of a copper horn

When Sal and Herbie burst into the kitchen, both filthy, the house rocks with an explosion of questions and news.

"You guys been mud-wrestling?" Phee asks.

"Dad!" Gabe grins.

"We heard noises upstairs!" Maria's eyes are still huge.

"Where've you been?" Phee gives her grandfather a gentle poke. "Really, Sal!"

"Thought we'd defend ourselves," Markus says, swinging his piece of kindling and whacking the rocker by mistake. It creaks back and forth wildly, as if insulted.

"Sorry," he mutters to the chair.

"You guys got ghosts, no doubt about that," announces Paul.

"We do?" Sal asks, winking at Phee.

"Ones that don't stay in the graveyard," Cyrus adds.

After the kindling is returned to the stove pile, Herbie leaves with all of the kids but Phee. He'll see them safely home.

Once alone, she and Sal plop down by the fire.

Both sigh with relief at the same moment, just as an old copper horn suspended on a hook by the back door clangs gently against the wall. The horn is part of a long line of hanging pots, ladles, and other metal doodads, as Sal calls them. It doesn't look as though anyone has used it in a long time.

Sal stares at it thoughtfully. "Now, *that's* odd. One of Flossie's favorite toys, that Crier horn," he says. "Used to belong to old Billy Clark. He was around when I was a kid, and that man loved to play tricks. Told the news but also fed the flues. Made things up. I used to blow it for your mother when it was time to come in for dinner. We should polish it up one of these days. It'll shine fit to sing. Horn must've liked the news of you kids sneaking around with ghosts!"

This Crier grins!

"Maybe someone wants us to use it," Phee suggests, not at all surprised by the idea of something old in the house having ideas of its own. "I mean—I *don't* mean for Flossie, not like it's needed, just . . ."

She then tells Sal about the what-if whisper of someone speaking her name and the rumpled quilt in her mother's room upstairs. Plus the hated book falling, the dresser, and the click of the door latch opening on its own as the kids went back downstairs.

Sal stops rocking. He watches his granddaughter's face as she talks, then rubs his hands together, that dry sound that tells Phee he's thinking.

"A noise isn't a person. Sometimes it's meant to confuse. Like smoke in a magic show. You'll sleep in my room tonight, my girl," Sal announces. "We'll bring your mattress in and make it cozy. The way we used to when you were little, remember? That way if there's any more bing-banging around here, whatever it is will know where to find us both."

Phee needs no convincing. After Sal blows out the candle that night, she rests quietly in the dark, listening to her grandfather shift on his crunchy horsehair mattress. *Like smoke in a magic show.* She loves the way Sal makes everything okay. Then she hears him sit up. He listens to the nighttime quiet for a moment and then creeps on bare feet past his granddaughter and out of the room. Phee hears him try the latch handle on Flossie's closed door.

Click-a-click! He tries it again.

The door is locked from the inside. This was something he'd always allowed his daughter to do, as she'd been afraid of ghosts as a child.

Phee now hears Sal whispering, "Flossie! *Pssst!* Is that you?"

There's no response.

CHAPTER 36

A familiar roaring

Ghosts don't sleep while the living do, but we drift, treating the darkness like water. Some might say we soar like a crow, black on black, but I think our movements are closer to dreaming. They can appear solid when needed, and even leave footprints. Delicious smells. Sensations that confuse the living.

Some are physically strong, as you've heard and seen.

That night, I, Mary Chase, am suddenly aware of a familiar vibration. It's the same dreadful feeling that first rattled me back from my peaceful rest in the walls of my home—a bone-deep roaring and shaking takes my breath away even though I have none. I sharpen my senses and wish with all my heart to be where I am needed.

This time, I don't ring or hoot. I concentrate.

I'm not in my home, that much I know.

Right here, a voice seems to whisper to me. *Right here*.

I find myself on the roof of an old house, its surface slippery with moss. Looking down, I recognize the yard.

In the distance, the roaring bobs between houses and trees, moving this way like an angry firefly.

Horn ready, I open my mouth and fill my lungs with air.

CHAPTER 37

A screeeeeeam!

Phee is awake.

The moon is perfectly round, and as she peers up at it, she remembers how it used to dance on the water outside the houseboat when she was very young. At times when she woke with a bad dream, Flossie would take her up on deck to see the gentle beauty of the night.

Phee settles her pillow, snuggling down, then pops to a sitting position. What is *that*?

The room is vibrating, as if a big machine is at work. Not nearby, but close enough. And over the distant roaring, she hears . . . a *screaming.* A woman is howling as if she needs to wake the world.

Here is a steady flag of sound, flying windless beneath a startled moon.

Hardly aware of what she's doing, Phee is soon up and dressed. She tiptoes down the stairs.

Outside, the roar is louder, grinding and bumping over the cobblestones on Main Street. Phee also hears the loud, frantic ringing of a bell.

Right here, she calls out. *RIGHT HERE*, as the words of her old game with Flossie fill her head. Now she sees children running toward her.

Coming from all directions, the kids are every size and shape. Some she knows, others she doesn't. And there is Gabe! He's racing toward her, next to a boy in a straw hat and a girl holding a doll.

On his other side are the three children from Pine Street, who are somehow recognizable. They arrive higgledy-piggledy, hair on end, jostling others. Maria, Markus, Paul, Cyrus, and Maddie are right behind Gabe, who waves energetically at Phee as if to say, *All here, all good.*

They *did* it, Phee realizes with a sigh of wonder. The Gang managed to lure out a whole bunch of kids, some from the houses that were mostly gutted. Dozens now pop over fences and from behind the old stuff in the Folger yard, like *a murder of crows*, she thinks, untroubled by the thought.

A chase of kids! The words pop into her mind from nowhere.

Then Phee sees the hulk of an earthmoving machine, one without its headlights on, rumbling closer. She recognizes it: one of Eddy Nold's bulldozers! Help, oh, *help*! What is he doing? The ground trembles under everyone's feet.

The howling is louder now and the sound comes from above. Phee looks up, puzzled, and sees a *woman* on what's left of their old roof walk, one with ankle-length clothing, her profile sharp against the moon. Her head is thrown back and her mouth open. Who *is* it and how on earth did she get there?

I watch myself through Phee's eyes right now, and love this moment. I ring, I scream, I glow with all the glory of a ghost who is heard and seen!

Startled awake, crows circle the house, their cawing slicing the night air like so many knives. I feel safe in their company.

Ages ago, Sal nailed shut the hatch door to the roof. He explained to Phee that the railings had rotted and it was too dangerous to be out there. Phee pictures the woman tumbling down, and her stomach jumps. Where *is* Sal?

The bulldozer turns toward the house, and the

headlights click on for a moment, as if to check location. In a rush, Phee understands.

Eddy Nold has come in the middle of the night to knock down their house! To stop the uprising of ghosts at his other sites by getting rid of Sal and Phee's home!

Adding shock to shock, Phee now sees light stream clear through the bodies of the children standing just in front of her, kids she doesn't know. Blink! The light goes off again, leaving the crowd once again solid and shouting. Phee wails also.

She and the rest of the Gang need more than the help of ghosts.

Phee yells, "*Saaaal!* Wake up! *Mommmm!* Where are you? Hurry, oh, hurry!"

And it's then that she sees Sal rushing out the front door. Next, she hears the slap-clatter of heavy boots running from all directions.

Herbie vaults over a fence and into the yard and, finding Gabe, stops in front of his son. He nods his head in a way that says many things: *You knew it before I did* and *Great job* and *I understand now.* Gabe returns the nod in reserved Pinkham style and then throws both arms around his dad's middle, giving him a quick squeeze. Herbie looks goofy with pleasure.

Soon the Folger house is surrounded. Phee sees Sal

give Eliza Rebimbas's shoulder a pat and then turn toward a young woman who looks similar to Flossie—her grandmother Polly? An old man with wild hair peeks out of the kitchen door. Phee thinks she recognizes her great-grandfather, Sal's dad, looking pleased. Soon, neighbors from all over fill the sidewalk in front. Phee knows a few as recent buyers in the area, others as longtime residents. No one seems surprised that some are flesh and blood, others not. Everyone's mouth is moving.

Big hands hold little hands. Old hold young. Handwoven coats and shawls mingle with modern jackets. And—can it be? Phee now touches Flossie's hand, and somehow it isn't sad—it feels wonderful. Her mom's hand, warm and true!

But how can this be? Phee's soul drops and then hits a dark surface. She is lost before something begins to reel her in.

At that moment, Phoebe Folger Antoine realizes that even if her mom is dead, she's *not.* Not, not, NOT! Flossie's *here,* RIGHT HERE with her girl, and that is all that matters! Right here, at home where they both belong. Phee feels her heart fill and then spill over in all directions, and suddenly she's hugging her mom, her face buried deep in her shoulder, her cheeks wet with tears. Hugging her so tight she'll never again disappear.

The screaming, cawing, and mishmash of voices stop suddenly as the bulldozer is switched off. Phee raises her head, wiping her cheeks with a sleeve. Eddy Nold climbs very slowly out of the cab.

"Well, I'll be," he mutters, looking at the crowd around the house. "I give up. Please . . . please forgive me. I didn't understand. I thought the house with the doughnuts was the only one . . . I didn't believe my dream. The kids who came to see me in the hospital . . . I should've paid attention. I thought I could stop all of this craziness by, well, giving your place a nudge in the middle of the night. I knew about all the old wood piling up in back and didn't think anyone was living here. Stupid of me, I just thought that because the place is so old and dark—Well, I'm done. No more trouble. Done."

Phee, to her surprise, realizes that Eddy Nold is talking to *Flossie*. Her mother now straightens her shoulders, crosses her arms on her chest, and says quietly, "Good to hear your thoughts, Mr. Nold. Odd way to take a spin on a moonlit night. Let's pretend that's all it was."

Eddy nods gratefully, shakes his head, then pulls himself back into the monstrous machine, his movements clearly painful. The bulldozer grinds in a slow semicircle and heads away, the roar retreating into the darkness.

Flossie thanks the flesh-and-blood neighbors who ran from their houses. She looks at the children already melting back across fences and slipping into shadows, but only mutters something softly to herself. Phee, realizing her mom is distracted, takes over and gives the Gang and all those other kids a grateful wave as they head off.

She wants to introduce her Old North friends to Flossie, but that can wait.

Phee and Flossie sit on the front porch steps in the dark and study each other, absorbing every detail. Phee's eyes glitter like stars and Flossie's hair clip sparkles beneath the moon. Soon, Sal joins them, and the three hold hands as if they'll never let go.

Sal lifts his head as though someone has called and hops up to meet that same young woman who looks like Flossie. The two of them slip sideways into the night.

Phee and Flossie get it. "Must be your mom, Polly. They missed each other," Phee says. "Like you and me."

"We did it," her mother murmurs.

"With a lot of help." Phee grins. "The kind of help that won't go away." And right then she realizes with a thunk of certainty that certain connections, ones made from love and belonging, don't break. They *don't go away.* Like the connections in the Folger family, she thinks, those between Sal and her grandmother Polly, or those between Sal, his daughter Flossie, and his granddaughter Phee.

Even if Flossie's not alive, Phee knows now that she is *here.*

~

Phee Antoine is right. And I, Mary W. Chase, am proud to know this.

What I've realized tonight is that we humans all need one another, although most of us don't see that while alive. Or dead! I thought before tonight it was just we ghosts who are swept around by change, but no—the living also ebb and flow like the tides.

Some swim and some struggle. None of us are the same souls we were a moment before, just as no splash or ripple in the ocean ever repeats.

From up there on the rooftop, I spot Aunt Thankful down in the yard, and we wave happily. She is old, and raises both arms toward me, her face shining with an approval and joy I never saw in her before. I blow my horn and ring my bell like mad, feeling as proud and wild as the wind. *Wind?*

"I'm back," it whispers in my ear. "Back, baaaaaack!"

"Wiiiind!" I shout through my horn, and yell so loud and long that it flies from my hand, turning end over end and falling below.

My grip relaxes, I wriggle my fingers and am glad. I sink to my knees on that mossy roof, exhausted. The crows are gone.

Perhaps it's time for another Crier.

The Old North Gang managed to work with little old me, a chase of kids, a murder of crows, and a once-heartless developer and, in doing so, changed us all. They tipped the island.

I'm headed home.

CHAPTER 38

Wind plus snow

As Sal settles back under his blankets, there are sounds from farther down the hallway.

Rattle-rattle! Plink, plink! "It's my old chicken-bones-and-dried-beans game! The one with scallop scoops! Remember that bowl with all the pieces on my shelf? The game I played with my dad! I *remember* that sound!" Phee whispers, scooting closer to Sal's bed.

He reaches out and pats his granddaughter's back. "This is just a change in the weather. Whoever is in there won't hurt your things," he whispers back. "Let's get to sleep. Maybe it's the wind finally coming up."

And as he speaks, that is exactly what happens.

After a month of utter stillness—one of the strangest Nantucket Novembers on record—the wind is back.

Whooooooo! it seems to be saying. *Whoooo toooo?*

Across the island, people of every age snuggle deeper under covers, relieved to hear the familiar buffet and swirl. Windows and doors rattle in their frames. Islanders sleep better than they have in weeks. Their dreams blow and drift, adding weight to the snow that deepens on front steps and chimney caps, sparkling beneath a wintery moon.

Wind plus snow erases angles, softens corners, hugs the old, and quiets the new. It whirls and blurs, rising in whipped-cream peaks. By the first rush of dawn, the island is a sugary landscape simply waiting for a wonder.

I'm talking about a *wonder*, the old-fashioned dough-nut kind.

First peek, then find! Beware and behold! Early crows are gathering in the tree nearby, dark ink on white paper, wings fanning.

Hide your secrets, all that's shiny may fly! Just now the message for my horn is gone, blown across frost-feathered glass and around empty houses, or what's left of them. It's icing the beach grass and pebbles. It's cupped in my open palm.

Fill your hands with snow and the diamonds of dreams! Quick, for I am tired and there is much to do.

CHAPTER 39

Kind hands and broken hearts

December 1.

The woman stands. She is dressed in a long, seaweed-colored skirt and nubbly sweater, and her hair, dark with streaks of gray, is rolled into a bun. She wears no jewelry aside from a pearl earring in each ear, softening the sadness around her eyes and mouth.

"Thank you for coming tonight despite the unseasonable blizzard. As many of you know, I was born here. As were my parents, grands, great-grands, and so on—I'm one of those! And I returned just over a year ago, after several years away. I returned to my home, yes, but also to unspeakable tragedy. But then again, tragedy is something my loved ones have become quite good at.

"Quite good—" She pauses, ducking her head. "What I mean is, many untimely deaths have happened in my family. My father refused to allow this ache to stop him. He believed with all his heart that it is up to those of us living on this island to reach out past our own concerns and help those who can't build a life here on their own, and to do it while protecting the beauty of our old ways." The woman, gripping the podium in front of her, pauses and swallows.

The crowd is silent until someone calls out, "Go on now! You tell it! Tell it for the children!"

The woman raises her head, ignoring a lone tear that rolls down the side of her nose, catching on her lip. She continues, her voice now stronger. "I speak of a beauty built by hand.

"Sitting next to the wood-burning stove in my family's home today, I appreciated what was around me. I rocked, watched the light dancing on old floorboards, the glow of new snow outside. I thought about what to say to you. And I sensed—oh, yes—that I wasn't alone. Let me say that better—I'm *sure* I wasn't alone.

"I think many of you will know what I mean. And because I wasn't alone, I felt even more clearly that my life is a *continuation*. Yes. I am carrying forward an idea. I continue the work of my daughter and father, but also the work of many island families. Folks like you and me who join together to enable dreams, and to stop some of the—the—*unfortunate* things that have become the norm among a number of homeowners in recent years."

Here the woman pauses and looks around the room.

"My heart is broken, yes, but I am also proud. And there is time. Time to work on fixing and safeguarding the treasure that is Nantucket. We cannot undo our mistakes, but we can carry forward some thinking that was begun by people we loved dearly."

The woman stops. "Yes, I'll say it: I think they are still here with us. There's no other explanation—"

Here she breaks off again, her face crumpling. A sob is followed by a hum of sympathy, the squeak of folding chairs, the stir of feet and jackets.

Pulling herself together, the woman clears her throat. "My heart is broken, yes, but I am also proud."

Splashes of applause ripple through the room. "I speak now as a preservationist, someone who is armed with a recent degree that I hope will serve to do good.

"Anyone can look at an old building on this island and see history come alive. Many of us who grew up on Nantucket believe that we live with ghosts, but it is more than that—our seventeenth-, eighteenth-, and nineteenth-century structures themselves tell stories.

"They frame the past.

"They carry it into the present.

"They *embrace* all lives lived within them.

"They bear witness.

"They breathe.

"Some say Nantucket has the greatest number of pre-1850 houses of any residential community in this country. I am lucky enough to live in my family's creaky old home, one that was built centuries ago, but any one of us in this room can rub shoulders with the past no matter where we sleep at night. What's gone is all around us. We can see it, visit much of it, and lay a hand on this same wood or brick almost anywhere in our town.

"That may not be true forever.

"During the past few years, there are newcomers who have bought historic houses of ours that they then practically destroy—truly, I believe, through ignorance of what is at stake. It's not malicious, just unknowing. Wanting everything in their homes to feel new and fresh, they toss most of the old. They enjoy the *story* of Nantucket, but they don't want to *live* with it. And in the way they've seen the island—or *not* seen it!—they have endangered the very soul of our town.

"Nantucket was long an outpost where folks who used everything at hand could build a home and live. Working people were the untitled kings and queens, tolerating visitors but setting the rules. We did things our own way.

This island was a place where money was neither the bottom line nor a recipe for happiness.

"I don't mean to sound like a grumpy native. I know that some of our recent property owners have supported the preservation of Nantucket's buildings inside and out, please don't get me wrong. And many of them have done extraordinary and deeply generous things, especially with land conservation, the arts, and adult education.

"But!" Here the woman holds up both hands. "That doesn't change the fact that we're facing a crisis here.

"Together, my daughter and father started a group called Nantucket Hands. They gathered many islanders together, families who do physical work on-island, some of them new to the United States—and introduced them to longtime Nantucketers who care about the island's legacy and future. Sal organized outings on land and sea." Here the woman breaks off again, and grabs for a tissue.

Her voice trembles as she continues. "My father and daughter wanted to make everyone welcome. And yes, to offer a hand."

She pauses. "My heart is broken, but I am also proud."

"You tell it, girl," shouts a man at the back. "You always did!" This brings smiles.

"No details now, Tony!" the woman calls back. "Don't you dare!"

A quick grin fades as she looks at her hands, rubbing them together as if with soap and water. "When I got the terrible news about the accident and rushed home, I felt as though I'd never find the strength to go on. But here I am. Here are all of you. We who live here are resilient people, souls who do not give up. Am I right?"

The room roars.

The woman repeats, "My heart is broken, yes, but"—and here the room picks up her refrain, calling out, "I am also proud!"—"as a member of Nantucket Hands, I am happy to say that no more of our old houses will be gutted in quite the same way. Too many are now watching: During the past year, we've reached news feeds of all kinds. We've had enough ghostly drama to satisfy even the most skeptical. We've been able to trumpet our message loud and clear. And when, the other night, some of us heard a bulldozer roaring through town in the middle of the night, we all made it to the right spot at the right time, and the right thing happened because of it. We were not alone in that. I know we weren't.

"Do I pretend to understand how this happened? Do I pretend to understand how building materials and tools were moved during the past month and accidents were caused? I don't. Any more than I pretend to understand why certain things happen in this life and others don't.

"But now for what's around us in this room." The woman looks up. "Thanks to the Historical Association, we were invited to put together a Nantucket Hands show, and this is it. And, I should add, we didn't do it without some *unusual* assistance.

"While setting up this show, a harpoon fell out the front door of the museum when one of us who had carefully taken it off the wall heard a knocking and, holding the harpoon, unlocked the entrance. Strange but true, this large weapon escaped from our hands and then floated right back in on its own. And a few of us have, well, *collided* with the invisible. We've brushed a piece of clothing, felt a touch, heard a footstep or a word. Four days ago, right over in that doorway, several of us heard a child's voice say, 'Look!' clear as day."

The woman pauses for a moment, rubbing her arms as if cold. "Of course, I called and reached out, but that was the end of it. Suddenly, there was nothing in that spot. Such is our island community, am I right? Something is there, and then it's not."

"You're our girl, you know it," a voice calls from the back.

"Thanks." The woman tilts her head and frowns, as if to guard against too much emotion. "And I hope I always will be. No more off-island for me! But back to what we can all share. Before I turn you loose to explore our tribute to the glories of useful things made by hand, and by everyday folks . . . I want to dim the lights and show you a happy picture. An image of some people whose lives mattered a great deal. This was taken a little over a year ago, on Halloween afternoon."

The lights go down and a huge photograph fills a screen on the wall.

There they are.

Gasps and moans fill the room.

Lined up on the deck of an old offshore fishing boat—*ding, ding!* prepare yourselves!—I see:

Phee. Sal. Gabe. Herbie and Becky Pinkham. The three Coffin kids—Paul, Cyrus, and Maddie—and their grandma Sue. Maria and Markus Ramos, their mom and their dad, Ray, who was Eliza Rebimbas's great-grandson. One of the teachers from school, the one who spoke with Sal. A handful of other islanders you haven't met, faces seen outside the Whaling Museum on the day the harpoon flew out the door. Many hands hold fishing poles or small hurricane lanterns.

The woman at the podium calls in a shaky voice, "We'll never forget them."

Now from across the audience comes the sound of open weeping. Here and there a voice calls out, "Never!" and "You bet!"

The woman goes on. "We all look back and wonder what we could have done to prevent this. The what-ifs and whys are endless. And Ghost, Gabe's dog, still returns to the beach every day, waiting for his master.

"Here is what helps me most: I hold tight to what Nantucket Hands is all about.

"It began in the heart of my daughter, Phoebe Folger Antoine, and she and my father, Absalom Folger, built on her dreams. My dad wrote to me that when she started school, in first grade, Phee worried about classmates who needed a place to live. Soon she and Sal were taking people into our family home on Main Street. That went on for years.

"Starting a few weeks ago, old but sound lumber being torn out of historic buildings around the island began magically to leave the dumpsters at 'renovation' sites and reappear in the Folger yard. In *my* yard. It seemed to travel by itself, and at night. Before it began drifting out to the navy base, the house was swamped."

Here the woman shrugs, her head on one side. "All I can say is that there are forces at work here, energies that no one living can explain according to the known laws of physics."

She takes a deep breath and swallows. "A little over a year ago, Phee wrote me a letter. On her own. And this, I must say, was a first; usually she added a line or two to her grandfather's letters. I'd like to share this with you."

The woman pulls a worn and creased piece of paper from her pocket. Hands trembling, she unfolds it and reads:

> *Dear Mom,*
> *It's time for you to come home.*

Here the woman's voice cracks and wobbles. "I can read this to you!" She tries to smile. "I can." A moment later, she continues.

> *We need your help.*

> *Sal is the best grandfather in the world, but he can't handle what's happening on his own. I don't want him to get hurt. We're kind of headed for trouble here, and I'm afraid Sal and I started it.*

Let's be honest: I *started it. I'm not sure now if that's a good thing.*

You heard about the new owners who want to gut old houses, and the contractors who do it. That is bad. You heard about Nantucket Hands. That's been okay.

Well, something scary is going on, too, something we can't stop.

EEK! I think all this destroying of the insides of old homes has woken up some ghosts that were maybe resting quietly before. I believe these spirits are trying to help us, but sometimes they seem more like they're having a tantrum at the same time. A few people have been injured, and badly.

You are a real Preservation Expert now. Can you organize something that will get the public to pay attention? I don't think anyone will listen to ghosts, Sal, or me and my group of friends, probably because some are invisible, he's old, and we're young. If you take charge of that side of things, of making a big noise that will get people to stop destroying our old houses, then maybe these house ghosts will step back and cool off a bit. Let's hope the work of Nantucket Hands can continue without anyone else getting hurt.

I know I sound bossy, but Sal says that you are, too. Sometimes that's a good thing, right?

I can't wait for you to be back in your old bedroom at home, the one between me and Sal. We've kept it dusted for you. I hope you'll get rid of Grimm's Fairy Tales. *Sal says it was his, I always hated it and he says you probably do, too. Full of nasty stories with sad endings. How about we drop it off at the Take It or Leave It?*

Love,
Your Phee

P.S. Sal sometimes calls me Fee-fi-fo Phee because I'm so determined and my ideas are giant. Hopefully that's good. He says you're pretty headstrong, too, and that you and I are two peas in a pod. I like that.

P.P.S. I miss you. I want my mom to come home. Please bring me some nice-smelling lip balm. Sal thinks that stuff is silly.

P.P.P.S. You belong here.

P.P.P.P.S. Hurry.

Here the woman blows her nose. After folding the piece of paper and giving it a quick kiss, she tucks it back in her pocket.

"So in honor of Phee and Sal, my life is now about continuing what they did so well. Their hopes and dreams are now mine, and that is what gets me up every morning. I want their work to become bigger than my sadness.

"Nantucket Hands is all about filling hearts.

"Filling hearts, finding homes, and protecting a certain historic side of this complicated, beautiful island. Everyone here tonight has the ability to do this for our loved ones—we can pick up where they left off."

A deep voice calls from the back of the room, "And maybe they'll help us!"

"They're not done, I know it!" a woman shouts.

"Too much spirit to disappear! Too much caring," someone else calls.

Flinging both arms wide as if to hug the room, her cheeks now wet again with tears, the woman calls out, "Thank you, Phee, Gabe, Maria, Markus, Paul, Cyrus, and Maddie! Thank you to Sal, and everyone else in the Folger, Pinkham, Ramos, and Coffin families, and to every other soul who was on board that day! Thank you to whichever island spirits wanted to help Nantucket Hands." Right at that moment, the clip holding her bun clicks open and her hair flies everywhere.

She reaches back, grabs for the clip, and waves it over her head.

Sparkly stars. "Here's to Nantucket! All hands on deck! And, Phee, *I'm right here, too!*"

The lights go on and the crowd surges to their feet, encircling Flossie Folger.

I'm at her side.

CHAPTER 40

Watch your step. Ding, ding!

I can't always see what's going on or keep track of who's doing what, but I do know that I AM STILL HERE to do a job, an important one. I believe that's because my house was recently rescued—and by a family who are in love with its oldness.

They saved me, me, ME. Mary W. Chase. Right at this tipping point.

I have to thank Eddy Nold, who has recovered from his injuries and become a leading force in the work of Nantucket Hands. He now has a business that truly *does* restore old houses! Proof that even the most misguided souls can change direction, he found the right family for my home. Tenderly, he propped up and repaired only what needed fixing. He told the new owners about Eliza Rebimbas and her famous wonders, and left them an old island recipe. They've done their best to honor her tradition. The plate she filled each day still sits on the chair by the front door, piled high each weekday afternoon. Children still stop by after school.

The painting of my aunt Thankful hangs in the living room. My old teapot is still on its shelf.

Claiming he was visited in the hospital by some of the kids who went down in the fishing boat, Eddy tells his story to any who will listen.

He freely admits that he was slow to believe in ghosts. In a fateful nighttime trip in a bulldozer, he almost knocked down the Folger house in a fit of anger at what Nantucket Hands had stirred up, but really at all whose love of old homes blocked his money-making.

In the process, he discovered the house was far from empty. He's still not sure what he saw and heard in the yard that night, but he'll tell you that he and Flossie weren't alone. He also found out that the neighbors cared.

Speak with Eddy yourself; you'll be glad you did. If you're lucky, he may even tell you about smelling a magical plate that was put down with a *clink* inside Eliza's empty house on a day when he stood outside.

That, for him, was the beginning of turning his head around.

A young girl who moved recently to the neighborhood near the Old North Cemetery takes the school bus from that stop. She reports that two boys, their little sister, and a set of twins sometimes ride with her—but the driver never sees them.

And look! Something to wonder at: Here, as a part of this very exhibit, is one of the old copper Town Crier trumpets. Up there on the wall, and so familiar! Now, *that* is something to blow, shout, and ring about! We Criers have always mattered on the island.

Sometimes I'm aware that Phee and Sal and Flossie are together again, and in the same room in their home. Although more's the pity, Flossie can't see her father and daughter, nor can they see her. They feel each other's presence, though, and are forever talking to each other. Flossie's always been one for speaking her mind. Phee, too. Sometimes I spot Herbie Pinkham around town, trying to do what's best for all, and I see the seven kids in the Old North Gang playing among the burial stones.

Here's a glimpse of the Folger household on a recent day:

Sal is studying maps at his table in the corner of the kitchen. Occasionally he notices the sheets of paper flap or shuffle on their own. Flossie is working on them, too.

Sal shakes his head and mutters, "That's my girl," at the same moment that Flossie sighs and says, "If you're here, Dad, give me a turn without rearranging stuff, okay? I know what I'm doing!" Neither hears the other's voice, but both are glad to be struggling with the other's company.

Before going to sleep each night, Flossie asks Phee how she's doing, and often she can close her eyes and hear a response. Phee helps her with Nantucket Hands by continuing to do the hard work of a ghost, and Flossie responds to her daughter by sending her nonstop love. They are close, and have a nighttime routine.

Flossie hears "Mom? I'm still your big girl, and I'm right here." And crazy as this is, Phee's voice sounds as deliciously froggy as always.

Flossie then repeats aloud, "Right here! *Right here!*" and feels peace wash over her.

The folks who went down on that boat are not gone, I can tell you. And oh, yes! What? No, it's true. *Not even one of us on this island is alone.* I mean *truly* alone. Not one. Ever.

I want to say a few things about broken hearts. Scars and injuries, I've learned by watching others, can change. Things *transform.* Take a tree. When it's chopped down and boards are cut from this dying organism, it seems like the end. But these same boards, after decades of being used in a home, fill with life again. And if they're then ripped out of that home before their time, there's another dying—but if they turn up in a *new* home, it seems there may be yet more living to be done.

And don't forget: The sea transforms the island itself and all who live by it. Day after day, year after year. Century after century. It gives and it takes. Shapes and reshapes. One kind of being becomes another kind.

Was there anything *good* about a fishing boat going down on that wild night and taking the lives of seven children, their families, and others who cared about our community? Certainly not. It was tragic.

BUT. There have been ghost stories around the world, in every language and century, for as long as people have experienced love and loss. What do these stories mean? Perhaps that none of us who live are ever truly gone or done, even when our time is up; that love is bigger than death; that beauty continues in what's left after life evolves—like a shell in the tide.

This quietest-ever of Novembers has turned out to be one of the oddest the island has ever known. One of the strangest and most bountiful. Even I have been surprised.

Never believe that what you feel but can't see isn't there, because it usually is. Never believe that passions or attachments die, because they don't.

And remember to join hands, as old Eliza Rebimbas cautioned.

She'd heard talk about the work of Nantucket Hands, and about Sal and his granddaughter, Phee, Flossie's little girl. Maybe Eliza wanted the church bells all ringing on the day she died in order to signal that she was on board. I think she meant to wake all who couldn't hear my bell and horn.

I do believe that many of us became deeper souls in that windless month. We were pulled from our everyday selves, whether living or not, by an emergency. If you had told me when I was alive that I'd one day die and later howl from a rooftop on Main Street, I would have run inside and slammed my door, thinking you were crazy.

I wouldn't have been able to imagine the beauty of that terrifying moment.

Lastly, call me outspoken, but I'll say it anyway: Watch your step, because you may bump into one of us.

Literally.

For heaven's sake, we're not trying to get into *or* out of your way! It's just that there are projects to be finished and situations to be stirred up, and we don't always put the spoon or the oar down with care.

We leave some of ourselves behind. This is true for

each one of us: the living and the dead. Didn't you know that? Words. A touch. Sounds.

What? Don't feel sad! From the perspective of a ghost on this island, I can tell you that we don't see the living as you folks see yourselves. Sure, being alive is wonderful, but it isn't the only kind of *being*.

A word of caution. Never forget that some of us are descended from those murderers who went out on whaleships, folks who executed both giants of the deep and, in a rough spot, each other.

And some of us who are dead aren't quite finished.

We watch. We listen. We warn. Sometimes we act.

But we can't control the currents that bleed the past across the present or the present into the past, any more than a human can control the sea.

Did I know, when I was spreading the news, that Sal, Phee, and everyone else in Nantucket Hands were not alive?

I didn't.

Did *they* know? Do they *now*?

Clearly not.

And if Flossie and her continuation of the Nantucket Hands group seem like ghosts to Sal, Phee, and all, *are* they?

Is there one kind of wonder? Or only one kind of ghostliness?

Again, I don't think so. On this island, the line dividing the dead from those still living is hard to find. Take it from me. And there are, I have come to realize, many simultaneous layers that fan outward over time, just as a tree has rings and a scallop shell arcs.

We ghosts can't always contact the living, nor can we control each other. But because we have nothing to lose—having already lost it!—we are free to do our best. Often that's far more than we did when breathing.

Beware! Shhhhh. The tide is coming in and that twist of shell by your foot—shaped from a sea creature once alive but now gone—may soon be washed away. Put it in your pocket. Store it in your soul.

And here, hold my hand.

Acknowledgments

Armloads of thanks go out to my husband, Bill, and to our family, who are a part of everything I write. Our daughter, Althea, shared an amazing true story about a crow and a young girl, which I promptly absorbed. Doug Klein has been passing along Shirley Jackson gems for years, and Mary Ann Dempster Klein gave me permission to drop the capital *D* on *dumpster*. My sister, Julie, found me ghost-catcher earrings and the crab shell with a wise face. My brother, Will, told me not to tone down this story. All have helped me more than they know.

Many hugs go to my friends in Chicago and on Nantucket for understanding when I needed to disappear into the book. I'm indebted to Paul Farrell for philosophy and Skip Hampton for footprints.

Many thanks to everyone at the Nantucket Historical Association Research Library for helping locate old photographs and recipes. I greatly appreciate seeing a number of nineteenth-century *Inquirer* and *Mirror* articles in the

Nantucket Atheneum Library Great Hall Reference Department.

David Levithan, my brilliant editor and friend, has once again kept me company from start to finish, diving into the world of ghosts and even supplying a scream at a critical moment. Doe Coover, patient friend and agent extraordinaire, has been enthusiastic throughout, reading many drafts and weighing in. Scholastic works as a family, and I can't thank all of you enough—especially Ellie Berger, Charisse Meloto, Lizette Serrano, my amazing designer Elizabeth Parisi, and the copy editors, whom I've no doubt puzzled to distraction. Leo Nickolls's cover painting is a beauty. The team is big, and I am grateful for every ounce of your creativity and expertise.

Nantucket residents' names appear, disappear, and reappear over the centuries. I tried not to borrow the name of anyone living. Please forgive me if I have. Any factual errors relating to the island's history, current statistics, and geography are entirely my own.

Lastly, I want to thank the ghosts.

OLD LANGUAGE

Here are the old Nantucket terms that appear in this story, in case you'd like to use them, too. Most started at sea and belong to the island's glory days, to the nineteenth century. There are many more in a 1916 book called *The Nantucket Scrap Basket,* a collection of stories and expressions compiled by an islander, William F. Macy.

at the helm: in charge, with the helm being the wheel, tiller, or other equipment used to steer a boat.

bow on: head-on or face-to-face, the bow being the front of a boat.

everything drawing: all working well on board, as in "all sails drawing" in a stiff breeze.

fair wind: a streak of luck.

fall to: to begin work.

gally: to frighten or terrify. Often applied to an alarmed whale.

greasy luck to us all: wishes for a good voyage with lots of whale oil.

grouty: grouchy.

heave ho: to pull with all one's strength, a command on board a boat.

keeping a weather eye open: looking out, staying alert.

meeching: mean, sneaky.

mollygrumps: low in spirit or down in the dumps.

muckle: to bother or disturb.

put out: to start, or to set sail.

running before the wind: lucky or in a good position; in a sailboat, being pushed forward by the wind.

scrimshaw: an image or piece of writing engraved on whalebone or whale's tooth ivory, then rubbed with ink to make it visible.

scud along: to hurry.

set sail: to get under way.

shooling: roaming about, in an unhurried way, looking for berries, clams, or some other treasure.

slatch: a bit of good weather during a storm, or a short time to relax.

taking a lunar: a look at the night sky, from the days of celestial navigation.

up scuttle: on the roof walk, a fenced platform also known as a widow's walk. The trapdoor to the roof was called the scuttle.

wadgetty: nervous or fidgety.

watch the pass: watch everyone going by.

whick-whacking: to dash back and forth.

ABOUT WONDERS

Fried dough is not the healthiest treat in the world, but it may be one of the most delicious.

Wonders have been around for centuries on this tiny island. Apparently the term arrived on Nantucket with some of the earliest European settlers—people that traveled from Devonshire, to the north of the Channel Islands, which perch between Great Britain and France. It was *those* islanders who first called a twist of dough a *wonder,* something so irresistible that no one wonders why.

Heather Atwood mentions this in her 2015 cookbook, *In Cod We Trust,* and she also supplies a Nantucket recipe for wonder-making. As the handwritten versions I've run across in the Nantucket Historical Association files are not specific about amounts of flour and other ingredients—or call for lard and "pearlash," an early form of baking soda!—this one is a find.

Nantucket has bakeries that make doughnuts every day. Hardly anyone gets more than a few steps with a bag of wonders intact.

I know I never have.

A Note from Blue

Nantucket is not just a location. There is a pulse. An awareness. Perhaps a response. This is something I've known for a long time.

Born in New York City, I first came to the island as a teenager, after high school. I waitressed and worked as a chambermaid, lived in a boardinghouse, and thought this New England outpost was the most intriguing, soulful place I had ever seen. From the moment I arrived, it pulled at me—insistent, a magnetic force. After college I came right back, on my own, to be and work and think. It was then that I heard my first Nantucket ghost stories. My husband and I met each other, fell head over heels, lived in a small house he built on a windy hill, struggled to pay our mortgage while two of our three children were born here—natives!—and then, over a decade later, it was time to go.

I worked to barnacle our island family to Chicago's world of skyscrapers and big signs and airports and highways. Urban parks and traffic. Sirens. A local diner where the undercover cops came to eat, wearing bulletproof vests. This was right, for many years. I knew how to do it, having grown up in a huge city, and grew to deeply love our Hyde Park neighborhood. I still do.

We filled our home in the Midwest with Nantucket scallop shells, large and small lucky stones, conch shells, horseshoe crabs, slipper shells—symbols found and kept. Treasures carefully carried away in pockets, boxes, bags. They landed in bowls and baskets, on shelves and by bedsides; Nantucket's jewels were everywhere in our home. Even after years in Chicago, if I needed peace, back I went, in my mind, for a walk on the dirt road near what used to be our island home, or perhaps a swim on the beach nearby. Early morning, pale water the color of celery, lemon juice, bubbled glass . . . into the line between sea and sky, the day slap-lapping and rich with minnows—a moment of pure delight. On the windowsill next to my writing table sits a large globe of a rock I had pried up from our dirt road when we moved. A stone rounded in the ocean thousands of years ago. One we passed over each time we came and went.

I guess it's obvious. A part of me remained rooted on Nantucket. A dictionary for the spirit, that's what this island is, packed with images that mean more than a person can absorb in one breath: shadows caught by the dusky bayberries that cling to a twig, calligraphy left by beach grass on wind-smooth sand, the poetry of cloud plus sky.

I first heard ghost stories on Nantucket a very long time ago, and collected many through interviews with an unlikely assortment of people, all of whom shared an experience they'll never forget. I've wanted to write *Out of the Wild Night* for decades, but had to meet Mary W. Chase first. Most of the details of her life that appear in this story are fiction, but Mary was not. She died in 1917.

Why Nantucket has so many ghosts is anyone's guess, but I do know they're here.

Photographs

NANTUCKET

1.1 *Streetscape, late 1800s, courtesy of the Nantucket Historical Association*

1.2 *Mary W. Chase in front of her house, late 1800s, courtesy of the Nantucket Historical Association*

1.3 *Cobblestones, old house and roof walk*

2.1 *Crier's horn*

2.2 *Old North Cemetery*

2.3 *Door in snowstorm*

3.1 *Old house lifted for basement dig*

3.2 *Old outside, new inside*

3.3 *Window with old glass*

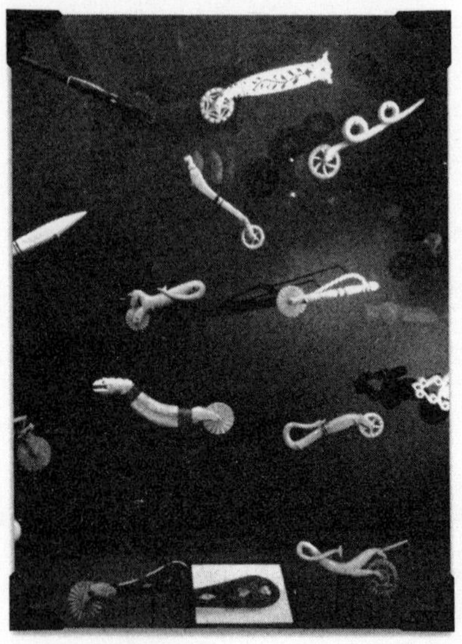

4.1 *Jagging wheels*

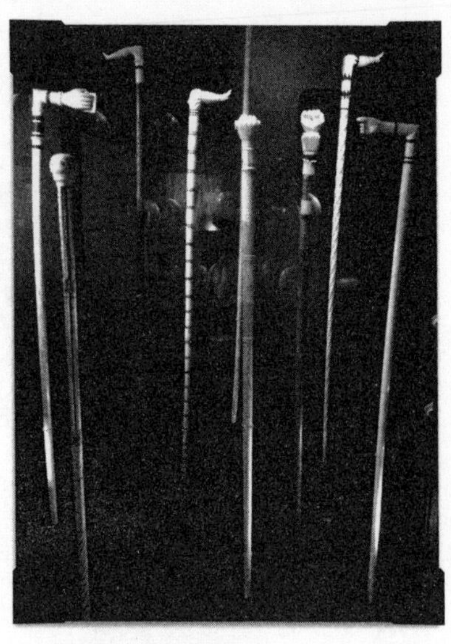

4.2 *Walking sticks*

4.3 *Whale's tooth and shells*

The Crier's horn, jagging wheels, and walking sticks are all a part of the Nantucket Historical Association collection.
Photos by Blue Balliett and Bill Klein unless otherwise noted.